"At one point…I was almost certain I was reading a Raymond Carver short story I had never read before. Apple (like Carver) is a writer of characters. He paints portraits with well chosen words. He understands his characters. Like many of the dirty realist writers of the '70s, Apple writes about small town life, the lower-middle class, the lost or conflicted, but in *Approaching Twi-Night* there is always a glimmer of hope."

— *H. B. Schooley, Amazon Reviews*

"Apple's writing is at its best in the extended play-by-play descriptions of individual games (sportswriting, like middle relief, is an often undervalued skill), including the culminating double-header referenced in the title, in which he effectively conveys not only the mechanics of play, but also the psychology of pitching…An overall solid effort; readers will find that it's worth sticking around for the last pitch."

— *Kirkus Reviews*

"*Approaching Twi-Night* really touched home, brought back so many great memories of my own experience as an owner and manager in minor league baseball. Most major league players will definitely be able to relate, from cramped bus rides to not having a lot of meal money, but just enjoying the game of baseball."

— *Ben Bernard,*
President & General Manager, Glens Falls Dragons (PGCBL)
Former manager, Glens Falls White Sox &
Albany-Colonie Yankees

Approaching Twi-Night

M. Thomas Apple

Kinoshita Kajitsu Press

New York / Kyoto

"C'mon, four-eyes, pitch it in here!"

"Yeah, four-eyes…four-eyes…four eyes…"

John squinted, peering into an invisible strike zone next to the batter, his brother Craig's friend. Waving an old beat-up metal bat ominously. T-shirt on the ground for home plate, surrounded by four or five classmates. Backyard ball.

Hiding the ball in his glove until the last minute, bringing up his left knee as high as he could, John reared back and threw.

"What the…?!"

KaCHUNK. The ball smashed into the chain link fence behind the batter, who had dropped the bat and jumped backwards.

"Friggin' Jew, you tried to kill me! He friggin' threw at my head!"

"Hey, settle down, he didn't mean nothing." Craig, defending him.

John threw his glove down on the damp backyard grass. "I'm not Jewish," he said, clenching his teeth and making a fist.

"Threw at my head…"

"Did not! That was a strike, right on the inside corner."

"Bullshit! You're a dirty Jew!"

"Told you, I'm not…I ain't Jewish. We're Irish Catholic!"

*Sneer. "Irish Caaaatholic, that's why you got so many kids."
Gesturing at classmates. "We all know what the Klein Daddy
and Momma been up to lately, uh huh." Gesturing at crotch
and pumping with both hands. "Oh, more Kleiny babies, more
babies."*

*Seeing red, John charged. Smashed into, dumped to the ground,
fists flying. Kill you, kill you good…Hands prying, pulling
apart, pushing, shoving.*

"Jesus, friggin' spaz, get 'im offa me!"

"Hey, John, cool it!"

"Ain't a Jew, ain't an Irish…"

*Glasses, where are the glasses…here, on the ground, bent
sideways but not broken. Someone holding him from behind,
two people pinning his arms at his side. John felt his bottom lip
protruding, swollen, knuckles bruised and aching. Left hand,
not pitching hand. Lucky.*

*Nobody spoke for a few minutes. Just breathing hard, staring
each other down. John swallowed, looked down, shoved his
glasses on his face again. He'd get contacts. No more glasses.
Sat crookedly on one ear.*

His brother's friend glared, then shook his head, spat, shrugged.

"Whatever. You ain't never going to the majors, Jew-boy."

"Hey, Thor, ease up…"

"Coach says…"

*"Coach? He's washed up. You're lucky he gave you a start.
One. You'll see."*

You'll see…

1

As he stretched his legs in the slowly dampening outfield grass, Ditch didn't need to watch the early evening misty June rainclouds roll down from the low mountains surrounding the Upper Hudson Valley to know the images they could evoke: scenes from a James Fenimore Cooper novel, the lower Adirondacks-sheltered small city of Gladden Fords and nearby growing suburbia, harsh dark brown squatness softened by warm breezes of the transition period from spring to summer. He grew up here, between ancient rocks and rapid river, among the ever-increasing middle-class housing projects which sprang up in bunches where Chingachgook once pursued Magua and cannon smoke filled the skies. The gentle ever-green mountains surrounded the local communities like strong mothers' arms, isolated clusters of families who never moved away, estranged from the sprawling capital city region of the state only a thirty-five minute drive straight south.

Now Ditch craned his head toward the sound of soft thunder. Small patches of darkening wispy fog were slowly invading the protected valley like the vanguard of a larger army to announce the storm's imminent arrival. He straightened from his self-imposed exercises, cracking his abused back and pulling his sore right arm then his left over his head. The old ballpark was quiet today, a mere two days before the start of the Class A short-season. The other players from the first-year minor league affiliate had already gone to their apartments or hotel rooms, satisfied with one last, shortened team practice. Ditch knew he needed more. He also knew it was too late to do anything about it now, even after the extended camp in Florida, after his last chance to play in the majors during the strike as a replacement player. As a scab.

He liked to think of the wind sprints as penance.

Ditch lowered his arms, removed his new blue vinyl baseball cap to spit on and to flex the padded inside rim. He remembered the last time he stood on this field. A senior at the local high school, playing the traditional last game of the season under the night lights, playing on the same field as the then-resident White Sox Double-A team, pitching a long, Pyrrhic victory in front of his parents.

The cap refused to yield. Ditch threw it to the damp grass in mild annoyance and stomped on it with a cleated foot. He ran his fingers through his short henna-brown hair and turned his face upward, closing his eyes to the mist. He hated new hats.

What would it be like, he wondered, to pitch in this ballpark again after nearly a decade of bus trips and disappointment? His parents would make it a point to be at the home opener, he knew, but he couldn't guarantee them he would play any given game. Not any more. That was the problem being a relief pitcher: any game, any time, he might be called on to throw to a few batters, and then go sit on the bench again. Occasionally Ditch liked to imagine he might start a game, like he did in high school, start pitching in the first inning and not stop until the very last. Grip the raised red seams with determination, mow through the opposing lineup, leave a smoking hole in his catcher's mitt, a row of zeros on the scoreboard and a big fat W in the scorebook.

As if it had actually been that easy.

Ditch opened his eyes. He no longer felt like doing wind sprints in the soggy outfield. The clouds had begun to pour into the valley, echoing thunder and rising breeze promising stronger showers. No point in running around exhausted in a downpour, not when the next day was the first of a week-long road trip. He flexed the trodden cap's headband, vainly trying to break its spirit before tugging it back into its uncomfortable place. A final scan of the recently-painted brown stands around the park, and he headed towards the center field gate, toward the clubhouse. It was time for a hot shower.

Dressed in his civvies, Ditch paused in the gravel parking lot to look back at the field. Under the graying dripping windy sky, the ballpark looked even more decrepit than under bright rays of day. The light towers which stood in the middle of the stands on all sides of the park all were missing a few bulbs, the square bullhorn-speakers outdated by at least twenty years, simple wooden benches for seats; even the ads on the outfield fence were in tatters and referred to companies that hadn't been in business since the late '70s. The city had barely improved the park in the years after they lost their minor league teams. First the Sox left, then the Tigers. Teams refused to play even exhibition games, leaving the community eight years without professional baseball because the city council was too cheap to fix a leaking clubhouse ceiling and a cracked concrete floor, too cheap to paint plywood dugout walls or to replace sixty-year-old rusted lockers. And all they needed was a surface coat to be in business again.

Houses lined the streets to the left and right; the park itself seemed to meld into the forested area beyond the outfield bleachers. Tall maple tree branches whipped around the lone Marlboro Man high-in-the saddle ad just inside the right field foul pole, guarding the swaying mounted cowboy and his pack of John Wayne cigarettes high above the drowning field. Ditch turned away from the wind as his sweatshirt fluttered away from his gut.

He pulled the lower elastic band down again around his waist, but it popped up again so he held it down with his thumbs as he trudged across the quiet cracked pavement, past the silent dirty-yellow Greek Revival houses to the next intersection. Five blocks to the center of town, to his apartment, or to his bar; he chose the apartment this time and fifteen minutes later flipped on the kitchen light switch.

While the coffeemaker percolated water for hot chocolate, the kid's drink he preferred over coffee, Ditch raised his right arm over his head, stretching the shoulder muscles, flexing the finger joints, testing, always testing. Tell him he had a bum arm, he grumbled to himself, what did they know? It'd just been a string of bad luck, that was all. Even the broken finger hadn't lasted all that long, a few months each time. It'd been bad timing to come early in his career, but a single broken finger didn't mean he was washed up. At least he hoped so, even if the Rangers and the Orioles didn't like him. He just didn't fit their program. Playing for his third major league affiliation this April, he thought he had finally made it; this April of 1995, Jonathan "Ditch" Klein would have pitched in major league ballparks as a replacement player, would have been in the record books, listed for all time as a 25-man, full-season rostered major league player.

Would have — but now the strike was over, and he was thrown all the way back to Class A, short season, even, with a new team, a young team, another chance. He supposed he was lucky, telling himself, *Third time's the charm, third time's the charm.*

He was staring into the bathroom mirror, a hot cup of cocoa balanced at the edge of the sink. Staring at his hairline — *was it receding?* he wondered. No, it couldn't be, he hadn't hit the big three-oh yet. *Not yet.* Staring down the hard lines indenting his cheeks, the stubble along his jaw and upper lip he still hadn't gotten used to because of team facial hair restrictions, Ditch wondered again, again and again, why he still played. *How many teams was it now...eight, ten, fifteen...*no, he figured it out in his head, the Wildcats was the eleventh. Eleven teams in eight years, going on nine. Eleven major-league-affiliated teams needing an extra pitcher who didn't mind five or six days' rest between appearances, didn't mind a couple thousand bus ride miles and twice-a-day fast-food meals to throw a single inning in an already lost-cause blowout with recent high school and college grads who were only going up and up while he stayed stuck. *Why?*

His writing forearm itched. He hated it when it did that. It acted up once in a while, more often recently. Whenever his twice-healed ring finger ached in cold weather, that he could ignore, but this itch he couldn't.

His body knew when it had to write, even if his mind didn't want to. *When you know you need to write, and you don't do it, you're just asking for a minor rebellion.* Ditch took a careful sip from the cup and discovered it was already beginning to cool, so he chugged it. Now there was a small knot of hotness between his lungs, right above the sternum, slowing working its way down between his ribs and towards his belly. He ignored the belly, easier than to ignore the itch.

Ditch went back to the kitchen for another hot chocolate packet and made the mistake of spotting his writing notebook on the black plastic covered couch. His left hand made a grab for it but the rest of his body managed to duck around the kitchen table and angle for the coffeemaker. *Dammit,* he thought, *if only I had a real apartment, with real rooms and real walls and not a cheap one in an old concrete and steel complex, I wouldn't have to pass the couch all the time.* He deliberately let himself get distracted by the answering machine at the far end of the kitchen countertop, back towards the outside hallway door, right beneath the generic, dull yellow, rotary-dial phone-on-the-wall. He poured hot water over the packet's contents and hit the message button:

zrrrrzzrrrMMMMEEEPPbeep "...Hi, John honey, it's your mother, listen since you're in town this weekend why don't you stop by for a little while you know your brother Craig will be home to see the home opener in a few days I don't know what the schedule is like but..."rrrrzzzrrkerk "...know you don't like Father Dennis but you really ought to go to church more often especially when you're..."

zzrrrmmmmmrrrkmmbeeP "...Hi, Ditch, it's Mike. I don't want to pressure you or anything; I mean, this is a favor I'm asking of you. not a job or anything. But I think you'd really like writing a column of your own. I think you're a pretty good writer, even if you don't. You're really too hard on yourself sometimes. I've read your stuff, and I think it's just fine. C'mon, give it a try..."

Ditch slowly stirred his cocoa.

"...well, you've got my number. Better call me at work...I'm usually there anyway...let me know, soon. Later."

The machine clicked and rewound as Ditch erased the messages. He tossed the spoon into the sink. It settled into the murky bottom of a stubbornly-crusted pot. He ran more hot water into the pot, a couple squirts of lemon-scented detergent as an afterthought. He turned the faucet off and placed his hands at the edge of the sink, looking out the square kitchen window. Even from here he could almost see the ballpark, the tall lights standing guard among the wind-whipped trees. He thought he could spot the silhouette of Mr. Marlboro, standing tall with his lasso high over his head, daring the wind to knock him down.

Ditch heard the spiral pages rustle. He looked over his shoulder at the couch and paused, the oncoming itch then propelling his legs into motion. He tried to will his right hand to shape a baseball but it resisted and came up with a broken-point pencil as his left opened the tan notebook. *Oh, no, not this part,* he thought, immediately turning the page over. He could never write a novel, certainly not finish that one — only ten pages long, and he knew it was done for. The pages flipped through short stories, all about baseball. Here was one: *no, not this one, this one was really bad.* And this: he had no right to pretend he was a third baseman, or any batter. The last time he was at the plate he practically ran away from the ball.

Who did he think he was, he inwardly griped, the next Mark Harris? *Uh-uh. Maybe Kinsella. No, no way, too mystical, too weird. What did those guys know about the minors, anyway?* he thought. Their heads stuck up in the clouds, the Yankees and the Cubs, *the great winners and losers, anyone else...Yeah, that's it,* he would just be Jonathan Klein, himself, as if he were the only person with that name, as if that name signified a destiny of greatness. But, he vowed, he would be remembered, he would.

He tapped the pencil against the arm of the couch; no, it was broken. *Where's a pen...ah, here's one.* His fingers paused above a half empty lined page, thinking, thinking. An idea forces the point down, nothing comes out, the fingers sworl in the margin circles of increasing darkness. They dip again and trace the image on the page word by word, building up an inky head of black steam. *I think maybe I've got something here, please...*The phone rings mid-scrawl.

Ditch drags the notebook to the counter, still tracing.

"Hello? Yeah, hi, Mike. Uh huh, I was just going to call you. Listen..."

2

John knew he came from a somewhat abnormal family.

Not that any family was "normal," he supposed, but, to be honest with himself, he knew that there just weren't very many families any more that had as many as four children, let alone seven like his. And he was the oldest.

His family had been moving around Upstate New York ever since it became a family. His father, a 20-year-old community college graduate at John's birth, once worked for the DOT. When John was three or four, with his Grandma Betty on a bus to the downtown Troy Atrium shops, he saw his father standing by the side of a busy intersection, holding a sign of some sort, wearing shiny orange and yellow clothes and a dirty-white hard hat, while larger men with plaid unbuttoned shirts exposing white tank-tops operated heavy machinery behind him. A short, slender man among the giants.

When the family grew to four children, they moved outside the Capital District to the "countryside" of

Albany County. John's father no longer worked on the roads, spent some time in a shoestore in a rundown plaza on Route 7, and then finally got a desk job at Oh Dee Heck. John was never quite sure what the name meant, or what it was all about, but his father seemed a little happier, even if he still wasn't able to spend any more time with his family, sometimes not home until well after John's bedtime.

Upon reaching six children, John's family made the final move to Gladden Fords. An old friend had offered John's father a desk job at a small paper mill in the Adirondacks. The job didn't pay much, though it was more than a night shift job and came with few health benefits, but John's father accepted it gratefully. He had started to put weight onto his five-foot-six frame and was plagued by a bad back. A new desk job he could handle, and he began taking accounting courses by mail to accommodate the demands of the position. Moving on up.

And where was John's mother throughout this? Barely out of high school, she had started working part-time at a local grocery store as a cashier while taking night courses at Hudson Valley Community College, where she met her soon-to-be husband. She decided to quit it all when John was born. She was 19, possessed a quick temper and in the early years occasionally beat

John and his brother Craig around their small apartment with wooden spoons and plastic wiffle ball bats. More than once while trying to sleep on the top half of his and Craig's bunkbed, John could remember hearing his parents shout at each other in almost hysterical tones. They moved to a bigger apartment in South Troy. Lisa was born, and the beatings stopped. John's mother began stealing change from his piggy bank to pay for gallons of milk. Luke was born, and they moved to Albany County. John's mother learned to drive and somehow the family afforded a second car to get groceries at the nearest supermarket thirty miles down the road. Ben was born, and they moved to Gladden Fords. Brian was born. It was 1979 and the Phillies were battling the Pirates for the eastern division title.

John. Craig. Lisa. Luke. Ben. Brian. And little Jennifer to come.

With his father's encouragement, in February of 1980 John decided to try out for the high school baseball team. He wouldn't turn 15 for five more months.

3

"Mike, what the hell did you think you were doing?"

Ditch rested the pay phone receiver against his shoulder, holding his copy of the *Gladden Fords News* spreadeagled in front of him, his Army-surplus green duffel bag at his feet. He half-listened to the local sports editor's reply, watching the bus warm up outside the clubhouse. He knew what Grant was going to say; he hadn't changed at all since high school.

"Look," Ditch interrupted whatever Grant had been saying, "Mike, you're making me out to be some sort of hometown hero cr something...which I'm not, and I don't have to tell you that...uh huh, yeah...and stop calling me 'Ditch,' okay? That was just a bad college joke the papers picked up on. I even got my Mom calling me three or four times, asking, 'What the hell does this "Ditch" mean?'...No, I don't think she reads anything besides the *GF News*..."

The bus was ready to go, the rest of the team already on board. The coaching staff, a few old fogies, outdated hitting instructors, and William Collins, the world's youngest manager, ambled out of the offices, grumbling at Ditch as he stood there next to the outside door, the outfield bleachers' overhang barely protecting him from the gray morning drizzle.

"Yeah...yeah...look, I gotta go. Four away games, you know, first couple in Oneonta, then in New Jersey...all right, talk to you..." Ditch hung up and thrust the paper under his jacket as he jogged out to the bus. The bus lurched to a rumbling start, closed its doors as soon as he hit the steps. Bouncing between the old green padded seats, Ditch made his way toward the back, imagined twenty-four pairs of eyes following him down the center aisle, thinking, *Damn, these kids look so young.* He found an empty seat half-way to the rear, across the aisle from the seemingly exhausted blond crew-cut catcher, Holforth, and plunked his bag down.

Holforth was the only one whose name Ditch could remember from spring training. Ditch had pitched with a couple of the other new Wildcat pitchers at the extended training camp at Port St. Lucie, but that was before anybody knew where they were going to wind up. At the time, Ditch had already been pegged as a middle reliever replacement player. The Mets had offered him $20,000 to play while the unionized regular players argued with the owners over money. Frankly, twenty-thousand bucks had looked pretty good to Ditch, but the prospect of playing in a big-league park was what really enticed him. To actually walk out the right-field bullpen in Shea Stadium, or to warm up along the foul lines in the Astrodome or in Wrigley, he would have played for near-nothing.

Then abruptly he was no longer needed. The owners agreed with the players at the last second to end the strike, handed the replacements $5,000 for their troubles, and banished most once again to eternal minor league careers. Ditch had been hoping for at least Class AA, Binghamton or Jackson, maybe. The last week in Florida, after learning he'd been optioned to Gladden Fords, Ditch had briefly lost interest in pitching. The new Gladden Fords team, those players who weren't still in school at the time, gathered on an auxiliary field to practice together for the first time. Altogether there were only twelve players of the team present in April. The Rule 4 draft for amateur players wouldn't occur until later that June.

Ditch found himself wondering if the team had simply been thrown together on the spot, as if someone at the front office decided they needed some place to put all their rejects. In the bullpen for his daily thirty pitches, he was the first pitcher that day to throw to a tall blond kid named Eric Holforth, the only catcher on the team at that time. Ditch proceeded to take his time warming up. Glove straight out, fastball. Glove out and back, straight change up. No fancy stuff. No pop on the fastball. He was bored.

And then Holforth had noticed the finger. After the second change, Holforth tucked his mask under his glove arm and walked the ball back to Ditch. "Hey, is your finger broken?"

Ditch stood still, glove poised to catch a return throw. "It was. Broke it twice."

The catcher placed the ball in Ditch's glove. "Lemme see it."

Ditch looked at the tall catcher, feeling short despite the added height of the mound. He shrugged, stretched his right hand before him, spreading the fingers. His ring finger bent slightly down and to the right, almost overlapping the pinky, a "dog-right," he called it.

Holforth snapped his gum. "Just like Cone, huh?"

"David Cone? He just got traded back to the Jays, right?"

"Yeah, he broke his pinky right before he got really good." Holforth smiled and put his mask back on over his helmeted head. "Cone started on the Mets, you know."

"Royals." Ditch couldn't help smiling sarcastically. "You gonna give me his career stats or something?"

"Hey, I'm a student of the game," Holforth replied, trotting back to the bullpen plate. He tugged his mask down firmly, covering his bottom lip and slightly muffling his voice as he instructed, "Throw another fastball and then a change. The change's looking funny at the end."

A big grin spread across Ditch's face as he wrenched his cap down to his eyebrows, like it was in high school. He gripped the ball cross-seam and toed the white pitching rubber. The three-quarter motion and big leg kick resulted in an audible pop in Holforth's mitt.

The next few weeks were monotonous. Throwing a couple dozen pitches every two to three days, intermittently dispersed between muggy days of on-field sprints and stretching workouts, live-ball fielding practice (especially covering first-base on a ground ball), and trips to the gym to do seemingly endless squats. He spent some time on beaches and even more time in beach bars the first two weeks before the pitching coach, Kriek, ordered him to go dry for a full five days. Stuck in "extended" spring training until the draft picks were assigned, Ditch was instructed to work on flexibility, particularly in his shoulders and upper back. The team was no doubt worried about his arm issues over the years; he figured, though, that it was mostly mental. Still, the workouts helped. He persevered.

By the time he was ready to fly north for the start of the short season, Ditch was in relatively decent shape. When the team finally gathered on June 20 to practice in their new-old park, the cliques formed quickly: high school graduates, college graduates, walk-ons and overseas signees. Ditch would have none of it. The team carried three catchers, including one catcher obviously destined for permanent bullpen duty, and twelve pitchers, but Holforth remained practically the only player he talked to. Most of the young pitchers had little experience working out of the pen in college, but he knew that as soon as the manager and pitching coach determined the starting rotation, the leftovers would quickly discover what the bench was like. He himself had learned quickly at that age.

The players stayed relatively silent during the three hour trip, the opening road trip of the young season. From Gladden Fords, the driver cut through Saratoga on route 50, intending to head west towards Ballston Spa and Scotia, then cross the Mohawk River at Schenectady before heading down Interstate 88 southwest through Schoharie County's "cherry valley" toward Oneonta, nestled between the Alleghany Plateau and the Catskill Mountains. It wasn't a smooth ride; starts and stops inside the cities, occasional bumps and ongoing road repairs would prove a challenge for initiates to the long-distance coach system of Upstate.

At first, Ditch stared blankly out the windows at the familiar faded brick buildings of downtown Saratoga, but he caught himself glancing around the bus, trying to identify faces. There was the bonus baby, Hansen, sitting by himself near the front. Hansen had signed for five million dollars right out of high school. *He must have some arm for that kind of money*, Ditch found himself thinking, jealously. Across the aisle Holforth had started snoring. Ditch glanced over his shoulder. The newly-tagged starters Dave Lawrence and Shawon White had their own copy of the *GF News*, and had discovered their names in Mike Grant's article introducing the team to the city fans.

"Hey, hey, look at this here," Lawrence laughed quietly, "we're already big stars!"

"Lemme see," White grabbed the paper and scanned the column. "Yep, that's me all...hey, wait a minute here! Dude spelled my name wrong!"

"Yeah?"

"Yeah! It ain't 'Shaon,' what kinda shitty name is

that? It's Shawon, you know, *ess-ayche-ay-dubya-oh-enn*, like my man Shawon Dunston."

"The man got my name right, homey."

"Talk to the hand, man. I don't gotta put up w' this, man. I'm gonna be a big star. I don't gotta take this shit from some redneck..." White flipped his cap around backward and took his headphones out of his ears. A few murmurs in front of Ditch rose in volume slightly. Holforth woke with a start and began rubbing his eyes, saying, "Keep it down, willya? Hard enough to sleep on this roller coaster."

"Hey, who this dude here? Look it all the space he got, man."

Ditch felt a sigh coming and coughed to exhale it artificially. He imagined White must have come across the lengthy, somewhat dramaticized version of his high school finale: a ten-inning game, lost when he let in two runs in the top of the last inning and could only get one back. Holforth gave a sideways grin and reached across the aisle to poke him in the shoulder. Ditch shook his head and slouched even further in his seat. He didn't feel like talking to anyone if he could get away with it.

Lawrence took the paper back, White rising and ducking out from under the luggage rack. "Hey," he called loudly down the bus, "who here this Ditch dude?"

A few short snickers, amused chuckles from the other players. *Man*, thought Ditch, *they must've all read the thing*. He half-stood in his seat, turned to face White. "Yeah, that's me."

White's face lit up, his amazed features hyper-exaggerated by arching eyebrows. "Man, you old!" Lawrence burst out laughing. Manager Bill Collins at the far front put down his clipboard of roster lists and schedules and turned slightly into the aisle. The bus bounced as it went around a turn, and somebody at the back cursed softly as a bag fell down from the overhead rack.

Ditch shrugged. "I been around."

"A few times, it look like," White guffawed, Lawrence following suit again. The front half of the bus was now awake, interested in this major league reject, the once and future hometown prospect in their midst. "This true here, you pitched ten innins in one game?"

Ditch shrugged again. "Yeah, a while ago."

"A while?" White grinned, stepping over Reynald's legs stretched across the aisle and taking a seat next to Ditch. "Man, I was just startin' Little League when you pitched that game!"

Holforth was awake enough now to laugh along at

that.

Ditch forced a smile, trying to relax. "Yeah, so that makes you, what? 19? 20?"

White smiled again. "That's right, man. Gonna turn 20 in a coupla weeks. One more year until I can drink..."

He paused dramatically, arching his eyebrows again, "...legally. I'll be an old man then, jest like my man Ditch here! Ha!"

A wave of laughter rippled from the middle of the bus outwards and back again. Ditch could make out a few words of laughter in Spanish from the small group gathered around Enriqué Aguirre, his soon-to-be roommate on the road. Ditch's command of Spanish was limited to "Cómo estás?," and his roommate's English wasn't much better than Ditch's Spanish. But at least he could communicate. "You call me Hank, si?" Aguirre had told him when they met, and shook hands. Ditch nodded. He really wished he could understand Spanish. At least this time, he thought with a chagrin, he could figure it out from the context.

The big first baseman Reynalds half-sat up from his prone position on the seats behind Ditch and Holforth. "Legally?" he snorted. "Since when does anybody give a shit about that?"

White looked hurt. "I ain't gonna drink until I'm old enough," he protested. "Against my religion to break the law 'n shit."

"Yes," Lawrence chimed in, "the innocent Christian youth of America solemnly obey the laws of the land. I assure you, I have no interest in the demon rum or watered-down beer."

Reynalds settled back, arms behind his head, grunted and closed his eyes.

"Ha!" White crowed. "Just listen to the brutha!"

"All right, ladies," shouted Collins from the front, "enough horseplay, and don't even think about breaking team regulations!"

Lawrence ducked behind his paper and sat straight upright with a disarming smile. "Don't worry, sir, we'll behave, sir." The quieting chuckles briefly erupted again, Collins smirking and jerking his attention back to his clipboard. White reached back laughing with an open palm for the five slap. Holforth leaned across the aisle toward Ditch and addressed him in a soft Tennessee accent, "So, Ditch, my man..." — in the seat behind, White mouthed "my man" very seriously, but Holforth didn't notice — "is this going to be like a Bull Durham kind of thing?"

Ditch pondered. "You mean, the veteran teaches the young'un, that sort of thing, or the kinky sex part?"

They laughed, a hormonally-youthful group laugh. Even Hansen near the front had turned around by this point. But he merely smiled, said nothing, grabbed his seat as the bus lurched again over yet another country road bump.

"This's the opposite, right? Pitcher teaches the catcher, right?"

Ditch pondered again, framing his chin with a forefinger and thumb. White leaned back and whispered "my man" to Lawrence and shook his head laughing. "Nah," Ditch finally said, "not gonna happen."

Holforth feigned surprise. "What do you mean? Don't you have anything to teach a young ballplayer like me?"

He couldn't resist that kind of a straight line. Ditch leaned forward to get everyone's attention and said as deadpan as he could manage, "Ain't no teaching some folk, homey."

"Ha! You aright, man, you aright!" White crowed, clapping him on the shoulder as Holforth shook his head. Ditch made a mock tip of the hat, starting to flip him the bird. He stopped himself, folded his arms and grunted. It just wasn't worth it. He didn't want to get all buddy-buddy with these guys, he didn't want to know any of them, and now they all thought he was one of them. That hadn't gone at all like he thought it would have.

He leaned back in the seat and looked out the window. Only another hour and a half to Oneonta. The bus had come alive, despite the sleepy complaints of Reynalds and a couple of others. White, Holforth and Lawrence jawed some more with random players chipping in. Hansen had already turned around to face the front again and put a set of headphones on underneath his cap, hands twitching to invisible drums. The bus shuddered and bounced.

"Will you keep it down back there?" Collins roared.

4

Hey, anybody home? John called out as he opened the door to his parents' house. In front of him in the short hallway lay a virtual army of sneakers and boots lined up on tattered newspapers. Through the doorway to his right he spied the large cabinet television which was tuned to a baseball game with the sound turned down. He heard the pattering of small feet and saw his five-year-old sister scamper through the dining room archway into the living room.

She took one look at him, stopped in her tracks, and fled back towards the kitchen without a peep. John closed the door and cautiously stepped into the living room. Mom?

A short woman with straight dark brown hair down past her shoulders came into his line of vision from the kitchen, wearing an oven mitt with a burn mark at its tip on one hand. John, is that you? She halted in the middle of the dining room; John's little sister had attached herself to her mother's legs. John's mother pried the arms away and scolded the squirming mass of reddish curly hair. Jennifer! It's only your big brother John! Don't you remember the photos we showed you of the two of you at Christmas?

John remembered. The pictures had been taken three years ago, the last time he had been able to afford the trip to Gladden Fords for the holidays. The previous time he had visited for Christmas had been nearly four years before that. Twice in the last seven years. No wonder the poor kid was scared.

Jennifer was looking up at John now. She crossed her arms and pouted. Go on, her mother coaxed, say hello to John.

Hi, John, Jennifer said curtly. You're not sleeping in MY room. She turned and scurried out the back door of the kitchen. John couldn't help laughing.

His mother gave him a hug. It's so good to see you again! Your father's out back in the garden with Craig.

John sniffed. Are you making cookies? he asked.

His mother nodded and walked back into the kitchen, still talking as if he were standing right next to her. Yes, well, with so many of the kids visiting for the game, they all go through them so quickly. Just yesterday I had two batches of cookies and now they're all gone!

Uh huh, John replied, wondering how much longer his mother would call her adult children "kids." Forever, he supposed. He followed his mother into the kitchen and paused in the doorway to look around. The clothes bookshelf was still standing against one wall, the clothes drying rack still perched over one of the floor vents near another wall, both full from his younger siblings home from college for the summer. The wrap-around countertop at the far two walls still remained cluttered with cookbooks and appliances and crooked wooden spice racks made in shop class. Go on out back and see your father, his mother said over her shoulder as she opened the oven door and pulled out a tray of slightly over-browned chocolate chip cookies. It won't be time to eat supper for another hour or two, but tell him he needs to get his rear in gear if we're going to have any bread to go along with the spaghetti.

Good old spagett, huh? John thought, heading for the back porch. He could hear his mother still talking out loud as if he were standing there. The back porch contained an old stand-up freezer and a small dresser, as well as Grandma Betty's old bed. It appeared as if the room John's father had created on the porch for Craig's summertime college breaks years ago was still in use by someone.

Opening the outer door, John noticed that a plastic

lawn bag had been placed over a fist-sized hole in the wall. I'll have to ask about that one, he thought, walking out into the backyard. The uneven dark green grass looked as if it had been mown in alternating strips, at different times of the week. The old swingset still stood to the right of the yard, just a few feet inside of an even older chain link fence held up with four by four wooden posts. John ran a hand along the top of the fence, rusted brown and bent at the tops, curled with age, past the spot where a crabapple tree once stood. He remembered afternoons in the fall, when, instead of doing his math, he and Craig would swat the little hard green apples with wiffle bats into neighbors' yards, over the backyard shed. The shed still stood at the opposite side of the yard from the swingset with chain link fences leading up to it from the house and continuing past it. The fence completely surrounded the yard, encompassing the third of an acre his family owned, the box of his past.

John found his father and brother near the very back of the yard, working in the patch of sand they called a garden. He skirted the stunted blueberry bushes which had replaced the failed boysenberry bush before them as his father finally turned around and noticed him. Dressed in a red, roll-sleeved plaid shirt and motor oil-stained jeans, John's father looked more and more like the middle-aged father of seven he was. He appeared to have aged dramatically since John last saw him, his hair white at the fringes, especially his beard, which had thinned considerably. He now wore bifocals, wide lenses spread across the upper corners of his cheeks.

John, there you are! his father greeted him, resting his forearms on a wooden rake. Sorry I didn't meet you at the door, I wasn't sure when you'd be stopping by. Say, I read they gave you number forty-one. Tom Terrific.

Somebody's idea of a joke, I think, John said.

His father gestured to the small patch of barren earth in front of him, a strip of sand between two beds of green beans. The sweet potatoes died on me again, so I decided to plant more beans. Only thing that'll grow this late in the season. He paused and mopped his forehead with his shirt sleeve. Craig still hadn't said anything, standing with arms crossed, wearing, along with a pair of Nike shorts and expensive red and black sneakers, the old T-shirt he always wore whenever visiting his parents.

Uh, Dad, Mom says we need some bread for supper, John said, putting his hands in his pockets. I think she means French bread. He glanced around the yard. He was standing in the indentation in the soil that once he and Craig had used for homeplate for wiffle ball games, a permanent trench in the lawn where their heels had daily dug for summer upon summer. He turned and faced the shed, which marked center field. To his right he could still see the mound he had built out of boards and dirt, now covered over by grass, as if it had never been there. The mound had doubled as first base for wiffle ball games, but the shed bore plenty of reminders of the mound's true purpose. The scars John had inflicted upon the back of the shed lay hidden behind random patches of weather-beaten plywood.

Well, let's see, what time is it, his father said to himself, drawing out his watch. Quarter to six. I guess I'd better get down to Grand Union before they close. I'll have to see if I can work on the garden after dinner. It won't be as hot then anyway.

He began walking towards the house. Hey, Dad, John called. How many are here now?

His father paused. Well, I think it's basically just you and Craig...and Jan. John raised an eyebrow at the unfamiliar name. His father glanced at Craig, then back to John. Lisa and her husband stopped by after the game for a while, but they had to go back to Syracuse...Lisa has to work early tomorrow...so... He coughed. Luke's at work until nine, and Ben and Brian are at a friend's house. Just the six of us tonight.

Huh, said John. Mom gave me the impression that there were a lot of people over for supper.

Well, your mother's memory is starting to go, I think.

She still goes through all your names whenever she calls Jennifer.

John's father walked towards the house at a slow even pace, the rake over his shoulder. John and Craig, both hands in pockets, slowly trudged after, their eyes intently focused on their footsteps. John debated whether he should ask his brother about the new woman in his life. Craig had already had one failed marriage and had moved to the West Coast back and forth twice since. He decided to clear his throat experimentally and try to talk without drawing his father's attention.

So...who's Jan?

Craig shrugged. We been seeing each other a couple of months.

What happened to...uh...Becca?

It's been a while since I talked to you, hasn't it? Craig shook his head. Been over a year since I saw her. Won't even talk to me now. He paused to spit, and shrugged. Probably better that way.

They were just outside the house now. John's father had shut the outside door behind him, like he always did, to keep the bugs out of the porch. John could see through the window in the door that the overhead fan had been turned on.

John stopped and thought for a moment. Craig stopped as well, turning to look over the yard behind them. So, John finally said, how long are you here for?

Just a couple of days, Craig said. Dad won't let me and Jan stay in the house together, so we had to get a room down at Motel 6. He paused to spit again. Bastard. He looked up at the sky and squinted. Sure would have liked to see you pitch today.

Yeah, well, that's the way it is for me. No guarantees for relievers.

Craig coughed. John said, Maybe if you stop by tomorrow night I might be out there. I'll see if I can get you some tickets cheap.

Craig shook his head. No, can't make it. We already got plans to go out up to Lake George, you know, go to the Great Escape during the day and then walk around the village at night.

John nodded, thinking there was nothing quite like the packed sidewalks of Lake George on a summer's night. Village of a thousand night clubs. Well, maybe some other time then, he said.

Yeah, Craig replied. They opened the door and walked inside.

The smell of chocolate still lingered through the kitchen and dining room. John could hear sounds of baseball from the television, and, walking into the dining room, he saw his mother kneeling in front of the screen, clapping her hands and trying vainly to make Jennifer interested in the game. Mommy, I wanna go ride my bike, she whined.

Good, good, her mother clapped. The good guys are winning.

Mommy...

Well, all right, but stay in the back. If I see you go out front there'll be no bike for a week.

Jennifer immediately tore through the back of the house. John suspected he would find the back doors left wide open in her wake.

His mother was carefully rising from her knees. Has your father gone and gotten that bread?

I don't know. Didn't you see him go? He came in the house before us. John turned around. Craig was pacing around the kitchen table, occasionally pausing to leaf through papers on the kitchen table. Um...where's...uh...

What's her name is in the downstairs bathroom, his mother replied, somewhat testily, John thought. Just then he heard his father coming down the stairs with a heavy sigh.

Jesus Christ! John's mother exclaimed. You haven't even left the goddamn house yet?

John slipped over to the television set. He looked at the picture frames hung on the wall behind the set.

No, I had to go upstairs and get my wallet.

Well, if you don't hurry up the damn store'll be closed and we won't have any bread for supper!

There's still plenty of time to get down there. It's only down the block, you know.

John's gaze wandered over a piece of old newspaper in a small three by five inch frame. He plucked it off the wall and realized it was a boxscore, carefully torn out from the *Dallas Morning News*, dated September 8, 1989. He quickly scanned the boxscore, down to the last few lines:

Texas	IP	H	W	K	R	ER
Guzman (L)	7.1	9	4	6	5	4
Klein	1.2	3	1	1	1	1

Frame in hand, he turned around to face his parents. Hey, Dad, look at this. He waved the frame in the air, and held it in front of him with both hands. I remember sending this to you.

His father smiled. I remember saving it, he said. And opening the screen door, he walked out to his faded yellow Ford truck. John's mother followed. John stepped out onto the front porch to see his father's truck rumbling out onto the street, a dirty white rag trailing from the ladder in the bed. His eyes followed the truck off to the left, where it disappeared behind a large oak tree. He lowered his gaze in time to see his mother stalking back from the sidewalk, a rusted red tricycle under one arm, Jennifer under the other.

5

"Jesus, Ditch, you think you could've been any more boring?"

Leaning back against the dark wood booth with his blue pitching jacket draped over the top rail, Ditch sipped at his brown ale, self-consciously brushing back a moustache that no longer existed. On the other side of the half-gallon pitcher, Mike Grant folded his arms across his red cotton tie and fastidiously ironed button-down white shirt. Grant's short curly-brown hair appeared meticulously permed and his silver eyes looked as sharp as ever. *That's right,* Ditch reminded himself. *We used to call him Dan, Jr. Even has Marino's chin.*

Ditch sniffed the air. Cigar smell from a couple of booths down almost made him wish he hadn't stopped smoking in college. His eyes drifted down the bar to the television set in the upper right corner. "Mike, you look like you belong on ESPN."

Grant kept his arms crossed and shrugged his shoulders to relax them. Ditch tried to concentrate on the

TV to hear the major league scores above the dull roar of the bar. Grant turned his head to glance at the screen.

"So, Mike, what's on your mind?"

Grant jerked his head back angrily. "You're still a wiseass, aren't you?"

Ditch shrugged and finished the glass. He reached for the pitcher.

Grant leaned forward and grabbed Ditch's right wrist. "Aren't you supposed to protect this hand?"

Ditch scowled and freed his arm with a growling twist. Grant let go easily. Ditch said nothing, lowered his eyes and finally grabbed the pitcher without resistance. He slowly poured the hazy brown liquid down the side of his glass, gently swirling foam rising from the bottom. He set the pitcher down with a thump and looked up.

"He deliberately used me last night, you know?"

Grant sighed, "Well, I don't..."

"He used me so he wouldn't be able to pitch me for the home crowd," Ditch said between swallows. He gripped the glass like a bat and moved it in circles on the table. "I got pounded after the first two outs, and he kept me in there. We were already down by five runs, and he kept me in there for three innings!

"So, of course," he continued, looking back to the far off TV, "I was too tired to pitch today. My whole family showed up for Opening Day, you know?"

"I know. I was there, too. I do live here."

Ditch nodded, raising the glass again and filling it again. He switched the glass to his left, slung his right arm over the top of his pew-like seat. "The only time I pitch this whole week, and I got wasted."

"So you take it out on my pages," Grant commented, slouching and cupping his once-filled glass before him. He raised his eyebrows questioningly. Ditch rubbed at his stubbly chin.

"Actually," he began, pausing to tip the glass a couple of times, "actually, I wrote the column on Friday, a day before my outing. I wrote it in the bullpen in 'Jersey. On the back of an envelope."

He tipped the glass again and abruptly put it down. "You know, just like Lincoln."

"What?"

"You know, how he wrote the Gettysburg Address...he wrote the Gettysburg Address while riding to Gettysburg on the back of an envelope."

Ditch laughed at his own joke and swallowed the last

of the glass.

"Ditch, what the hell are you talking about?"

Ditch slammed the glass to the tabletop. "DON'T call me Ditch!"

The two were quiet for a moment, Grant coughed. "John..."

Ditch held the pitcher poised, "Have another drink," and poured into the mostly full glass before Grant said anything. Grant held the glass between fingertips, reluctantly taking a sip.

"So," he tried, "what's the team really like? Any personality conflicts yet?"

"No way, pal," Ditch half-smiled, "I'm no snitch."

He poured himself another and quickly took a swallow. "Besides," he added, lowering the glass, "I don't really hang out with anyone on the team. They're just a bunch of kids. On the road they got me rooming with some Hispanic guy. I can't understand his English, and my Spanish sucks, so we get along great. The others...I dunno...it's like they think they can party every night."

"You always came to our weekend parties."

Ditch allowed himself another small smile. "Well, a

couple of times, maybe. I was never big into parties, you remember."

He quaffed the glass and reached for the pitcher. Grant motioned toward the almost empty pitcher with his head. "Aren't you going a little too fast? What about the team rules?"

"To hell with Bill's bullshit rules," Ditch snorted. "Anyway, they only apply to hard liquor. And I can handle beer, you know that."

"Uh huh, tenth grade. Remember that party at Monroe's? One of the 'couple' you went to?"

Ditch gave a little laugh and swirled his glass of foam. "Yeah, half a beer ball, four in the morning."

"Half, my ass. The whole thing."

They both laughed. "What was it I kept singing over and over again?" Ditch asked, downing the last of the ale. "Pressure...da dee dee dum da dee dum dum...pressure..."

"You never could remember the words, not even sober."

"Can you?"

They fell silent. The TV buzz broke through the

lowering murmur of the after-happy-hour crowd. The cigar smell began to recede, a final milky cloud of smoke wafting up to the hardwood beams.

"You still seeing that girl from New Hampshire?" Grant said suddenly. "The one you met at UMass?"

"Mike..." Ditch turned the glass upside down in a small pool of condensation. "I don't want to talk about it."

"Oh." Grant grimaced, playing with his unfinished drink. "I'm sorry, I didn't realize..."

"Look, it's just...maybe later, okay?"

"Yeah."

Ditch waited for an awkward pause to swell before reaching for his jacket. "Well," he started, coughing into a fist. "I gotta get going. Get my beauty sleep."

Grant stirred. "Yeah, right."

Ditch rose and thrust his right arm into a sleeve, removing his wallet from his back pocket with the left. Grant also reached for his wallet, but Ditch shook his head. "I got it."

"You sure?"

Ditch tossed a ten into the pitcher and pulled the rest of the jacket on. "Sure. Just finish your beer."

Grant stood and pulled down his sportsjacket from the coat rack at the end of the booth. Ditch zipped up and shoved his hands into his pockets as Grant tipped the glass. "No beer goes to waste around me," Ditch said, watching. He smiled humorlessly. Grant lowered the empty glass and pulled his jacket down from his shoulders, tugging at the lapels.

"Christ," Ditch murmured. "You don't look like Marino. You look like Gregg Gumble."

Grant smoothed his sleeves. "Yeah?"

The outside door opened and a small group walked in. Ditch turned toward the door, held it open with his foot. "See you around."

Grant nodded as he watched Ditch exit. The door closed. He took a step, paused, then reached into his inside pocket for a small notebook. He sat down at the empty pitcher and tapped the pen against his lip for a moment as a teenage waiter in a green apron wiped down the nearby tables with a dirty washcloth. He put his head down, and began to write.

6

He was an outfielder in 9th grade — though that didn't really mean much, since everyone in high school played a little outfield. Only the coach's favorites got to play the best positions, like shortstop, or second. Or pitcher.

John liked to think it was his skill and determination that won him a spot on the varsity team that year. Carter was in his last year in the White House, the Fat '80s loomed ahead, though no one knew it at the time, but John could have cared less about politics and the economy. All he cared about was that the Phillies this year were finally going to beat out the Pirates, and the Yankees were going down in flames. All John's friends were Dodgers fans, despite the fact the Orioles and Pirates were riding high in the baseball world. John didn't care; he had his secret allegiances, and the more he feared someone discovering where his true hopes lay, the more he cheered for whomever happened to be in first place.

That cold April, after late snow showers forced the

postponement of a week's games, John couldn't deny that luck made him a pitcher. The "ace" of their staff broke his wrist in a skiing accident, the last fling on the slopes before the snow finally disappeared and the resorts left their patrons with ice granules. Now the coach needed another pitcher for the fourth slot, moving up the three starters by one peg in the rotation. John jumped at the chance.

Had John ever pitched before?

Yes, sir, in Little League and even a bit in Pony League.

Could John throw a curve?

Yes, sir, he could throw a curve *and* a slider.

Did John think he could start a game every other week and go at least five innings?

Yes, sir, he believed he could, neatly completing the small series of lies. The coach bought it. You're starting in three days, he said. I want you to throw sixty pitches a day. Get going.

John won his first game in a rain-shortened five and a half innings, five to four. No strikeouts, no walks. The coach called him an athletic groundball pitcher. John supposed that was a good thing. It guaranteed him a starting role, at least. And he could still play left field. Ah, who cared if the Phillies were on top; John was flying high.

7

Ditch felt a hand shake him. "Hey, Ditch, Ditch..."

He blinked and shook his head. Seated on an uneven wooden bench in front of his open locker, Ditch had only managed to get his uniform shirt and his sanitary socks on. His glove rested on his bare legs, his cleats and pants next to him on the bench. Ditch turned toward the shaker.

Holforth. "Hey, man, you better come see this. Bill's pissed."

Ditch dropped his glove and followed Holforth out of the locker room to the field entrance. There, attached to a square bulletin board just inside the door next to the equipment room, was a single, thin newspaper article. Ditch read:

Home is the Hero?

by Michael Grant, Sports Editor

Opening Day at Old Field should

have been a momentous occasion for Gladden Fords; it should have heralded the return of baseball, and the return of the native.

But for the capacity crowd, despite the Wildcat's 8-3 victory over the visiting Oneonta Yankees, a hometown disappointment was in store: Ditch Klein did not pitch.

After signing autographs during pre-game warm-ups, why wasn't the local favorite even allowed one batter for the fans? According to the reliever himself, it was because of a managerial *faux-pas* over the weekend.

"He did it on purpose, didn't he?" Klein mused yesterday. "We were behind by five runs [on Saturday in New Jersey] and he left me in to take my lumps."

> Klein went on to question manager William Collins' intentions, whether Collins deliberately used him to avoid using him on Opening Day...

Shit. A swift turnabout and Ditch found himself pounding in socked feet through the emptying locker room toward Collins' office at the far end. *Shit, shit, shit.* Skidding around benches, he turned the final corner and banged on the office door as he reached for the knob.

"Look, Bill, I need to talk to you..." The door opened outward.

Collins stood behind his cluttered desk, charts in one hand, the previous day's statistics in the other. He didn't look up. "Klein, I don't have time for this."

Ditch stopped short. "But, I..." He swallowed and let his hands drop to his sides. "Look, I was taken out of context. That guy, he..."

"What?" Collins snapped his head up, glaring.

Meticulously dressed in suit, tie and hat once again, Collins seemed intent upon playing the throwback to the good old times manager. His recently clean-shaven face, in adherence to his own strict facial hair regulations, accentuated the deep lines beneath his eyes and down his cheeks to a prominent cleft chin. Ditch wondered if the manager had actually drawn in his facial lines to make himself appear older.

"Look, Klein," Collins spat out, "I'm in charge here, I'm the manager. I got people coming and going all the time, ballplayers missing their mommies and daddies, don't even know what lineup I can field on any given day…"

"Hey, look, I didn't mean…"

"…and the last thing I need is some over-grown teenage reporter from a good-ole-boy rag trying to second-guess me. And I don't need second-rate over-the-hill relievers blabbing to the press behind my back."

"But I didn't give him an interview, we're high school buddies, and he…" Ditch paused, his eyes narrowing, "…wait…did you just call me 'second-rate'?"

Collins calmly stared back, leaning forward slightly, clipboard in hand. "Let me make this clear," he said through thin lips.

"Did you just call me a has-been?" Ditch said louder and more slowly, beginning to tremble as he pronounced every syllable. He felt his hands forming fists.

Collins didn't budge. He leaned closer and repeated in a low voice, "Let me make this clear, Klein. I run this show. You pitch when I say you pitch. You try to disrupt this clubhouse, ruin this young talent, and I'll see that you never pitch for this team again."

Ditch clenched his jaw, forcing his hands to relax. Collins kept staring at him, as if daring a response. Ditch placed his hands on the edge of the metal desk and leaned toward the taller man. "You think you're intimidating me?" he grated. "Do you?"

"I don't need to intimidate," Collins replied in an almost monotone, remaining motionless. "You need to do your job, and stay the hell out of mine."

Ditch said nothing, locked his elbows.

"You got that?" Collins said, straightening. He tucked the clipboard under one arm, papers slipping from the clip and flitting to the floor as he attempted to tighten his tie smartly. Ditch relaxed and backed away a bit, crossing his arms, watching Collins suavely scoop up the papers and neatly tap them against the desktop before reclipping them. Ditch shook his head, deciding to back down before things got worse.

"Look, Bill...Mr. Collins...I'm not trying to take over the team. I had nothing to do with that column. I wasn't shooting my mouth off about you, I was mad at myself. I pitched like shit."

"You got that right," the manager said evenly. He still wore a threatening stance. "You pitched crap. Didn't matter how long I kept you in there, crap is crap."

Ditch shifted his weight and kept his arms crossed. The two of them stood there in the middle of the office, facing each other, saying nothing. Collins pulled his pocketwatch out and examined it. "You want to pitch, 'Ditch'?" he finally said, corners of his mouth showing private amusement at his witty rhyme. He looked up expectantly.

Ditch said nothing. He nodded slightly.

"All right, then," said Collins easily, sauntering past Ditch to the open door. He paused just outside the doorway and turned back. "You'll pitch. You'll pitch every chance you can get. Every game I can use you, any situation I can find, whether you're tired or not, you'll pitch. Your arms hurts, too bad, you'll get used to it."

He smiled. "After all, it's what your adoring public wants."

Ditch kept his arms crossed, his mouth closed, refusing to be goaded any more. The hat bobbed in mocking triumph. Collins pulled the clipboard from under his arm and pretended to leaf through the sheets.

He glanced up. "Well, get out there," he snapped, his eyes darting down briefly and then back up to eye-level, "...and put some fucking pants on." He banged the end of the clipboard against the doorknob and disappeared into the locker room.

Ditch resisted the impulse to slam the office door shut, knowing full well it would do him no good. He deserved this, he decided, even if his manager was acting childish, even if his old high school friend had gone behind his back. He held the twisted ring finger, flexed his right hand. The bullpen called.

Holforth was already warming up the day's starter, Hansen, in the open field pen along the right foul line. As Ditch walked across from the center field clubhouse opening through right field, Holforth said something he didn't quite catch. Hansen paused from his throws, opened his mouth to say something. Ditch shook his head and motioned to the backup catcher who lounged against the chainlink fence surrounding the field. Hansen looked down and kicked at his mound. The catcher walked over to Ditch and asked, "You just throwing a few, or is this like a serious warm-up?"

Ditch shrugged, pulling a worn browned ball out of his glove, practicing his grip. "Little of both, I guess. Start slowly."

The catcher nodded and turned toward the second pen plate.

"Hey," Ditch called, "what's your name?"

"Stanley," the catcher said over his shoulder. He reached the plate and stood, glove ready. "Frank Stanley."

Ditch cocked his arm. "You related to that guy on the Yankees, Mike Stanley?" He threw the ball in an easy motion. It drifted into the catcher's mitt. Stanley pulled it out and tossed it back.

"What?"

Ditch sighed, and reared back in earnest. "Never mind."

8

There was a knock on the door, and John jumped up from the couch to open it. Mike was still dressed in his T-shirt and sports jacket from work. He stuck out his right hand and smiled. John took it, and they hugged, a manly bear-hug with back-pats to the beat of the ESPN theme song.

Come in, John said. Sorry about the downstairs doorbell. I've called the landlord half a dozen times to fix it, but I'm never around long enough to make sure he fixes the damn thing.

He let Mike in then closed the door behind. Can I get you some coffee or something? I think I got some beer in the fridge, too.

No, that's okay, Mike said, looking around the apartment and trying to appear as if he wasn't. He glanced at his wristwatch. It's still too early.

John slipped into the kitchen. Never too early for a beer, he said, opening the refrigerator door and withdrawing a can of Hills Brothers. Coffee, then?

Sure, came the reply. Mike was still standing in the middle of the living-slash-dining room, hands in his jeans pockets. John watched through the kitchen partition, underneath the hanging wooden cabinets, as Mike took a few steps towards the open balcony door. John started up the coffee maker and called out, So, Mike, how's the wife and kids?

Mike smirked slightly and half-turned with his hands still in his pockets. I don't have any kids, wiseass, but the wife's fine.

Just asking, John shrugged, moving to the couch and picking up the remote. ESPN's major league baseball game of the week between the Dodgers and the Cardinals showed the score as the dugout camera panned through the seventh inning stretch home crowd in St. Louis.

John, Mike blurted out, look, I'm sorry about that piece in the paper the other day.

John shook his head. Don't worry about it.

I know I pissed you off, Mike continued. He glanced out the balcony, then hung his head. I heard what happened with Collins.

Yeah? From where?

Hey, I have my sources, Mike said. He paused. Look, I...

Mike, John interrupted angrily, just forget about it, okay? What's done is done. Just...just next time, don't quote me unless you tell me ahead of time, all right?

The ball skidded between two diving infielders and rolled into the outfield grass. An outfielder in a white uniform with blue letters charged it and pegged a throw to second.

Hey, John remarked. Busch Stadium's got real grass now.

Mike nodded. Yeah, didn't you know?

John didn't respond right away. Finally, he said, You know, if you want to tout me as a hometown hero or something, why don't you talk to my dad? I'm sure he'd give you some quotables. Or maybe get a hold of my old high school coaches or something. I think Fletcher's in Albany now.

No, Mike said. He's a high school principal in Oswego.

You're kidding, right? What are his qualifications? Three cups of coffee every morning on the practice field?

John tossed the remote aside and got up. He walked

over to the balcony and opened the screen door. There's coffee now, if you want some, he told Mike.

Okay, Mike said. He disappeared from John's vision. John grabbed an old green lawn chair and lay back, watching the clouds slowly unfurl across the bright blue late June sky. The last free afternoon at home for a couple of weeks. Might as well enjoy it, he thought. It'll probably be raining on the bus ride to Utica tomorrow.

There was a nudge at his left shoulder from a cup of cream-colored coffee with Mike's hand attached. Here you go, Mike said, letting John take the cup. Didn't know if you wanted anything in it, but I guessed lots of sugar and milk.

Guessed right, John said, taking a sip. He held the cup against his upper chest with both hands, feeling the heat through his threadworn shirt. Mike passed up on the remaining lawn chair and leaned back against the door frame, watching the steam from his cup swirl upward. The traffic from the nearby street mixed with the June bugs to create a swelling and ebbing drone of noise, punctuated occasionally by the drumbeat of a neighbor's rap music.

Nothing like a lazy June afternoon, John mumbled. He closed his eyes. Feels good to be outside on a day like this.

Yeah, Mike said, finally taking a sip from his coffee. He swallowed. Besides...um, I hate to tell you this, but...there's a...smell in your apartment, you know, a...guy smell.

What the hell are you talking about?

Well, you, uh, I mean, I never noticed it until after I got married.

What do you mean? John laughed. I clean my apartment, it's not like it smells like a locker room or something.

That's not what I'm saying. It's just...never mind, it's not important. Mike took another sip. So, he said slowly, what about this girl of yours?

John sighed. All right, all right. She's not my girl, okay? She, uh, we broke up over four years ago.

Wow, you have been away for a while.

Yeah, John thought. A lot can happen in a decade.

So, anyways, what happened? Mike asked. I mean, if you want to talk about it...

John opened his eyes and drank the coffee. It was getting a bit cold. Well, I guess I was expecting too much. I was bumming around the Mid-Atlantic League, and then I got the call up to the Show in September...

This was the second time? with the Orioles?

Yeah. Anyways, I broke my finger again, so I was done for the season. I decided to visit her in Boston. Turns out she'd been screwing just about everybody when I was away.

John paused and drank the rest of the coffee. He set the cup down on the balcony's wooden floor and folded his hands behind his head. I guess I was an idealist, you know? What do you expect, I was away for almost three years straight, not including the middle of the winter. I lived with her from October to January, but other than that, I didn't see her for three quarters of the year. You know that saying, absence makes the heart grow fonder? Well, it's ca-ca.

Caca?

Yeah, caca. Bullshit. Well, we never really had much in common anyway...

So you blame yourself, don't you?

What?

How many women have you slept with? Mike asked matter-of-factly.

John was taken aback. What's that got to do with anything?

C'mon, tell me.

Okay, one.

Mike sipped his coffee and made a face at it. He put the cup down and put his hands back in his pockets. You know what your problem is? You don't have any self-confidence.

Oh, really? Are you going to tell me what my college friends told me, that what I really need is a good lay? Mike, I'm Catholic…

No, I'm not going to tell you that. I just mean, Jesus, man, you're moping about someone from four years ago that you barely knew, and you complain that you don't have someone now, and all you do is whine about how miserable your life is!

John was silent.

I mean, I know you're a great guy, I know you, but what do people you don't know think about you when all they see is someone with a bad attitude? I mean, here you are, a pitcher in the minors, something some people would kill for, and you've got your own place, and you don't have any debts…right?

Well, yeah, John said reluctantly. I paid off my student loans a few years ago.

...and you've got a bachelor's degree and all, unlike me...

No, I don't.

Mike opened and closed his mouth without saying anything.

I never finished the four years at Albany, John said. I was told I would have a chance in the draft the middle of senior year, so I went for it, and when the Rangers got me near the end of the draft, I decided to jump ship. I meant to finish it up during the off-season, but I...I never really got around to it.

Well...you could still go back, if you wanted to, Mike said. I mean, look at me, I only went to ACC and here I am, a newspaper editor with my own staff.

You know, I probably should have just gone to community college, too, John said. And then transferred to Plattsburgh like everyone else and forgotten about baseball. Maybe I could have majored in marketing and gotten a real job and had a real family...

And then you'd be happy? Mike shook his head. You're a ballplayer. You have to play ball. And you know it.

Mike took a long look at his watch. Look, John, I gotta get going. There's a staff meeting in about half an hour, and then I have to make sure tomorrow's page is all set...

Hmmm, love those AP boxscores...

Uh huh. Look, you don't have to do the column if you don't want to. I can't make you, you know. But I still think you could do it. Mike slid the screen door open and headed for the apartment door. Where should I put this cup?

John grunted and got to his feet, stretching with a yawn. Just put it in the sink. I'll take care of it later.

He made his way to the door and opened it. Hey, listen, he said, sorry if I'm a shitty host. It's just...you know, I never wanted to be a hometown hero. I just wanted to pitch.

Uh huh. Mike smiled a little. Hey, we have to have somebody besides good old Dave LaPoint.

Yeah. But he made it to the World Series.

Only because he was a lefty. Mike shook John's hand. Let me know what you decide, okay? You know the number. The space is still open for the column this

Sunday when you guys get back from the road trip.

John nodded. Mike left, and the door closed. John walked back to the couch where the game was still on TV. The camera had zoomed in on someone in the crowd, a ballplayer's wife with her name in white letters at the bottom of the screen. She looked like a model.

He turned the TV off and went to listen to his answering machine messages again

9

From his perch on the mound, Ditch shaded his eyes and watched the foul ball gently curve over the grandstand toward the parking lot. As he held his glove out for the new ball, he could hear his father's voice from a high school game: "Straighten that out, Johnny, just straighten it out!" And he could remember himself at the plate, thinking, "I can't, Dad. I can't hit it."

He gripped the dull white leather in his pitching hand, tucked the glove under his left arm and slowly circled the mound. Ditch's hands worked the leather, trying to deftly massage life into the ball. His fingernails found the seams and began to pull them up from the leather; Ditch had always wondered as a kid why pitchers on TV wasted so much time walking the infield grass, if "raised seams" actually did anything to curves like his father claimed, if pitchers who stared out at the crowd were actually looking for someone. He stopped on the first base side of the mound and glanced at the runners on first and second, not really to check on them, just let them know he knew they were there. The runners strayed a step or two from their bags, sauntering back and forth with hands on hips, kicking the bags a couple times impatiently. They knew Ditch wouldn't throw, he knew they wouldn't run, not on Holforth's arm.

Ditch tugged at his cap and deliberately ignored the anxious hometown crowd on "Opening Day Two." Absently he wondered if his family was in the stands somewhere, his father holding little Jennifer up on his shoulders, pointing, "There's John, there he is." He climbed back up to the pitching rubber, haphazardly pulling his short sleeves up and shrugging them down again. The murmurs changed to a soft buzz of rushing air in his ears as he dug in with his right foot and stared in at Holforth behind the plate. He squinted on purpose at the flashing fingers, set for the third pitch, and threw.

The batter fouled it off again, this time straight into the visiting team dugout, nearly hitting the coaches at the top of the steps. Ditch received the next new ball and began his ritual anew. The batter fidgeted, stepping out of the box with one foot and nervously swinging his bat a few times and changing his grip as if he were uncomfortable using wood instead of aluminum. Ditch looked at the wispy clouds overhead, the one-two count in the back of his mind, and decided to waste a pitch.

Holforth almost failed to block the errant pitch, but he managed to smother the forty-foot curve, hurriedly flipping his mask off and alertly checking the runners back to their bags. The catcher turned to ask for time, and Ditch turned his back on the plate. Holforth was bound to be angry. He knew Holforth hated it when his calls weren't taken seriously. He tugged his cap and kicked at his trench.

The catcher pulled the ball out of his mitt and placed it in Ditch's. Holforth darted a look at the vacant right field foul line bullpen, then back at Ditch. "You can let go now," Ditch said. "I've got it."

Holforth withdrew his hand from the glove. "Inside and high," he stated. "This guy's never used a wooden bat before." He turned back to the plate and pulled his face mask on over his hard hat. *Neither have you,* Ditch thought, already pacing at the back of the mound, massaging the ball. He found the soft spot, brown from the last pitch. *The Majors spoiled their pitchers,* he thought. *They want a new ball, they get one.* Even now, he knew, a batboy was rounding up the foul balls in the dugouts and along the foul line, ready to hand them over to the plate ump between half-innings. He randomly glanced at the rust-green electronic scoreboard with the Pepsi label slapped on it in left-center field. A two-run lead he was supposed to protect, for the last two innings. Collins had made that clear; Ditch was on his own. He felt the urge to spit, then changed his mind, then did it anyway. *What the hell*, he thought, pushing his sleeves up again.

He stepped up again and caught the signs. High and inside. At the hands. He checked the runners, reared, and threw at the batter's head. The kid ducked as the ball flew at the backstop. He could hear Holforth's muffled curse as the catcher futilely flung his glove hand back and followed it with his body. Ditch loped to the plate to cover, but the runners stopped at third and second as Holforth got the ball back in play. Someone in the crowd behind third base booed, but his neighbors quickly hushed him. Ditch cleared the dirt around the plate with the tip of his shoe and tugged again at the hat. He headed back to his incantations. The infielders hesitantly moved back to their positions, pounding their gloves and muttering nearly inaudible words of encouragement. A hit would tie the game. Ditch let his sleeves fall down as he mounted.

Holforth was standing right in front of him. Ditch betrayed no surprise. "You're making me look bad, man," the catcher said tersely. He rubbed the sweat dripping down his chin onto a sleeve. "We can't do that again, so I want you to throw the pitch."

He shook his head and dug at the trench. Holforth called it "the pitch," as if it were a secret weapon of some kind; he wanted the awkward slider he made Ditch work on in the bullpen, the one he could throw with the bent finger underneath. He hated it. He hated using a trick pitch.

"I'm telling you, do it," Holforth repeated. "Cut the crap and get this guy." He turned abruptly and trotted back to the plate. Ditch placed his right foot behind the rubber and looked up. The other ump had moved to behind third base. *Only two umpires in this league,* Ditch remembered with a chagrin. He looked in at the plate and jerked his head back to third as he faked a throw. The runner froze, then looked embarrassed, realizing that the third baseman wasn't anywhere near the bag for a pick-off throw. Ditch smiled to himself and tugged at his cap with his ball hand. The third baseman edged towards the bag, pulling the runner closer. Ditch paid the two no mind.

He looked back in. Holforth signaled for the pitch. Ditch shook his head. Holforth signed for it again. Again, Ditch shook it off. Exasperated, Holforth audibly slapped his thigh. He angrily flipped down a single finger. Ditch laughed out loud. The batter called time. Ditch stepped off and put his head down. He could hear the plate ump say, "Let's go gentlemen." *Gentlemen,* he thought. *Yeah.* He watched the batter take a few more swings, adjust his helmet without adjusting it at all, and then step back in. The crowd noise briefly interrupted then seemed to recede.

He looked in and he saw Holforth stand up and adjust his cup before squatting again. Ditch turned his head to peer at the runners momentarily, then turned back and got the expected signal. He didn't respond. The signal came again, insistent. He lowered his head, and stood, hands ready at his belt. He could sense Holforth settling back, the ump crouching behind with a hand on Holforth's shoulder. The bent third underneath and two forefingers on the seams, he withdrew his hand from the glove. His wrist snapped out and down, and the ball spun towards the batter's waist. It seemed to rise and curve left, directly into the batter's wheelhouse, but suddenly it dropped to the right at knee-level. The batter swung.

Ditch looked over his shoulder as the second baseman scooped up the ball and lazily tossed it to first for the third out. He was out of it. He tugged his cap, maybe to acknowledge the smattering of applause, and walked to the dugout. He was vaguely aware of the fielders passing him, some smacking him on the back, some not, as Holforth appeared at his left elbow. "Told you," was all he said, then found his place on the bench. He passed his manager on the steps. Collins pretended to be absorbed in pitching charts. *Whatever*, Ditch thought. He found his jacket and shoved his right arm into the sleeve. The end of eight. Maybe he would get through this after all.

One of the starting pitchers approached from the left side of his peripheral vision: the tallish Hansen, the deposed starter of the day. Hansen looked tired, but not beat. He held a cup of water, and nodded towards the bench. "Mind if I sit down?" he asked. Ditch shrugged, watching a Wildcat batter, the first baseman Reynalds, take a hefty cut at an eye-level pitch. After Reynalds would come a second-string outfielder, Williams or something, batting as designated hitter in the pitcher's place. He was glad he didn't have to bat, the only good thing about the minors.

The kid sat down with a contented sigh and took a sip from his Gatorade cup. "Hey, you want any water?" he asked.

Ditch shook his head. "Nah."

"Lemme get you one." The teenager was up and at the cooler before he could say anything else. He opened his mouth and shut it after a moment. *Why not,* he thought. *Doesn't really matter.* Reynalds swung mightily at a pathetic curve and topped it back to the pitcher. *Just one more run,* he thought, *no, make that two, or three.* He moved forward, resting his elbows on his thighs as he pulled his cap off and worked the rim.

Hansen walked over and handed him a paper cup with rosin-stained fingers. The chalk clung to the green cup as Ditch mumbled a thanks and took a small sip. Hansen sat down again with a thump and said nothing for a moment. The DH was at the plate, wildly swinging at anything near the strike zone. Ditch sighed, thinking that maybe he should be allowed to bat for himself.

Hansen finally spoke. "Thanks for getting me out of that jam."

Ditch was silent. *What jam? Oh, yeah*, he remembered, he had inherited the first runner. He turned to Hansen. "Sure thing. I didn't help myself with that walk, but...yeah, sure."

"Hey, you're saving my game for me, right?" Hansen paused to finish his water and toss the cup aside. "I owe you one."

"You don't owe me anything," Ditch mumbled. "It's my job."

Hansen was quiet. The DH finally connected — luck, Ditch thought — and hit a worm-burner past the shortstop for a hit. Now one of the outfielders was up, somebody, he didn't know his name. All he hoped for now was that the batters took a few pitches and gave him a little more time to sit. The next batter swung at the first pitch and popped it straight up to the catcher. Ditch hung his head and spit at his feet as the third baseman Corrales took his turn batting.

Hansen coughed into a fist and shifted on the bench. The batter was taking his time. Ditch hoped so. Corrales was their "star player," according to friend Grant. In the on deck circle, Holforth was taking his practice swings with his chest protector and shin-guards on. Ditch sat back and pulled his glove on, half-heartedly to head back to the mound.

"Hey, Ditch," Hansen began. Ditch didn't take his eyes off the field. "Uh...some of the guys were thinking of, you know, hanging out after the game," Hansen continued. He shoved his hands into his pitching jacket and banged his cleated feet against the concrete floor of the dugout. He had knocked the dirt from his cleats the previous inning, Ditch noted. Hansen cleared his throat. "You know, like go out to a movie or something. You wanna, I mean, if you want to come with..."

Hansen let a breath out slowly and stopped kicking. Ditch finally looked over at him. *Jesus*, he thought, the kid was actually nervous just talking to him. "Yeah, okay, sure," he said. Hansen looked at him, then lowered his head and resumed banging his shoes. "Maybe we could hit a bar or something first, you guys don't mind."

The sharp crack of the bat cut off Hansen's reply. They both looked up to see the ball soaring straight up, a routine infield fly. The opposing team's shortstop didn't have to move as he gloved it.

"Well," Ditch said, dropping his jacket behind him, "back to work." He heard Hansen's voice say "...one, two, three..." as he bounded out of the dugout. He glanced over his shoulder and saw Hansen get to his feet and show signs of pacing. Ditch reached the mound and, stooping to pick up the ball, immediately dug at the seams with dirty fingernails. He mopped off a sudden downpour of forehead sweat and looked back to the dugout. Hansen was sitting again, his face buried in a hand towel.

Ditch waited until the first batter of the ninth slowly stepped in and paused to dramatically spit and flutter his bat menacingly. The crowd murmur rose and fell in waves as he readied for the signs. He wanted this game, he realized suddenly. A fine time to get sentimental, but he wanted to win.

Well, then, he thought, rearing back for the pitch. *Here goes nothing.*

10

John knew he had to answer the message.

Two days had passed since Vivian called, asking for directions to his apartment. On her way up to Montreal, she said, to pick up a few things at a...friend's house. Then down to Toronto, across to Detroit to visit her old grandmother, and then who knows where. Somewhere on the West Coast. She'd like to stop by for a visit, a stopover on the northern leg of the journey. Here; here was her home-away-from-home number, leave a message, she'd pick it up on the road from a pay phone. Be seeing you.

He knew he had to answer. He didn't want to. He had to.

She arrived at an overcast Friday noontime, the last day of the homestand, in a tiny red car packed with clothing covering the back windows. Through the balcony sliding doors he watched her pull into the back lot, but he waited until she had come around front and rung the buzzer. He greeted her with a forced friendliness, an awkwardness which attempted to conceal two feelings, one of nostalgic longing, one of unforgiving regret. She smiled and said she felt as if she'd been on the road for days.

He made her some coffee. John, Vi said, with some hesitation, is there anything I could eat? A bagel? A sandwich? She'd been living on pbj, she said, picking the mold out of her last grape jelly jar. He acquiesced.

She ate as they talked, carefully treading with conscious discomfort.

John mentioned to her that he had been writing again. But, he muttered, it stunk. It would never be good enough. It was crap. He was crap.

If you don't think you can write, she asked, why do you bother doing it? She put down her cup and pulled out a cigarette. Do you mind? she asked. Well, I don't have any ashtrays, he replied. I quit smoking.

I didn't know you ever did, Vi laughed, lighting up. He wandered over to the couch, picked up a random empty bottle from in front of the TV and thought: Two and a half years. We were seeing each other for two and a half years, and you don't remember that I smoked. He set the bottle in front of her, watching her tip the ashes past the lip, casually. She coughed briefly and lowered her head.

I don't have anything to say, he stammered, gripping the coffee mug with both hands. He took a sip and swallowed. Nothing new. Everything I want to write has been done before. Everything I could say has been done before, everything I think has been thought before. What else could I say? What could I write that would make any difference?

Why do you still play ball? she asked, standing up. He opened his mouth to respond to the non sequitur as she took a couple of steps toward the kitchen. Do you mind if I make myself another sandwich? she asked, cutting into his train of thought.

No. No, go ahead, he said, waving a hand. I don't know if there's anything left besides bread, though. I mean anything good. Things might have gone bad after our first road trip.

That's okay, Vi said over her shoulder. She had opened the fridge door, extracted the jam. She continued, I mean, you told me once you didn't think you were good enough to stay in the majors. So, that means all you can do is play and make numbers in the minors. You know, all those statistics, all those numbers, they've all been done before. You're not going to make it into the Hall of Fame or whatever. All you can do is make more numbers, right?

Stats. Vi had been a psych major, John remembered. Three years younger than him, when he first met her through a mutual friend in Amherst, an opposing pitcher. After an away game during a rainout makeup doubleheader, the second game a fairly good outing for himself, he was introduced to Vi at a party of some sort. John wasn't good at parties, never was. He just liked to drink and to watch the goings-on. She liked to watch, too, she said in a private conversation. The body is the physical manifestation of the inner person, she confided. You could tell what someone was like through careful examination of material context: gestures, gesticulations, mannerisms, intimate corporeal details of the anatomy.

He had believed her, then.

John brought himself back to his present, surreptitious peeks at Vi, standing at his kitchen counter, cig in mouth, purple-covered knife in hand. What had she told him, at the time? Fifty. She'd been with fifty. I don't want to be just another number, he'd told her that last time. She looked pleadingly. I can't help how I feel. I can't...

Fifty-one. How many numbers were there now? John wondered. He supposed she was right. There are no new numbers.

So, why do you keep playing? she asked again,

replacing the jar and tossing the knife into the crowded sink without a second glance. She took a drag on the cigarette, made a face, then tossed it into the bottle on the table. Don't know why I still smoke these things, she said by way of explanation. She sat down and reached for the remainder of the bagel. It's a filthy habit, really.

Well, John said, fiddling with the mug in front of him, it's a job. It pays.

There are other jobs, she said. She held onto her coffee cup almost in desperation. Without a cigarette, he surmised, she had nothing for her hands to do. You went to school for journalism, didn't you? You could get a job at a newspaper somewhere. I mean, if you wanted to. He said nothing. He did not want to mention the fact that he had not graduated, and that he had told her that years before.

She squirmed and stood, looking for her purse, which hung from the chair behind her. Slinging it over her shoulder, she grabbed the sandwich. Look, sorry I can't stay longer, but I'd better get going. I want to get to Montreal before it's dark.

It was nearly two. John nodded. He knew it was only four hours, tops, to Canada. It no longer mattered.

...and there's supposed to be a storm coming, she added. At least it looks like it. John got up and tried to look out the balcony nonchalantly at the cloud-covered sky. Yeah, looks like it, he said. He let her out of the apartment and walked her down the back stairs to the lot. Drive safely, he said into the passenger window. I'll be all right, she forced a laugh. Thanks for the sandwich. She sparked the engine to life. I'll send you a postcard when I get where I'm going, she promised. John nodded.

He stood back and watched her drive out of the lot. Reaching into his pockets, John found that he had forgotten his outside keys. Luckily, his neighbors never completely shut the front door to the building. He walked around to the front, pausing at the outside door as Vi pulled up to the stop sign down the street. She didn't see him, didn't look back. He forced himself to stand there until the car turned around a corner and was no longer visible. It took a slight tug to pop the door open, and John climbed the steps to his apartment.

He opened the door. The knife, the cup lay where she had left them. Picking up his own mug, he slowly emptied the dregs of the coffee pot into it and stirred in too much sugar, as usual. The sky appeared darker...no, he told himself, that's just me being the victim. Stop it.

He opened the sliding door to the early afternoon breeze. A few drops occasionally spattered the spreading lot beneath him, but they were only wind-blown from the faraway storm. Thunder faintly rumbled over the surrounding mountains, but there was no lightning visible, and the storm did not enter the valley. John sipped his coffee, twice, and then dumped the rest over the balcony. Consulting his watch, he closed the door and dropped the empty mug onto the couch, next to his open notebook. He considered the notebook, and decided against it. Less than an hour until the pre-game warm-ups for the night game. John knew he had to expect Collins to throw him again, rest or no rest.

He checked the answering machine. Two messages. The first from his mother, two days previous; the second, Vi's. He'd erase them later. Pausing only to turn off the coffeemaker, John headed out for the field, closing the door behind him.

11

"I dunno, man," White muttered, glancing around the dark room as the six of them sat at a corner booth. "This place don't feel too compftable, like nobody here never seen a brutha before."

Slinging his jacket over the wooden bench behind him, Ditch eyed the fake wood paneling and animal heads on the walls. They'd been bar-hopping for an hour and a half after the game, and everywhere they'd stopped had something wrong with it. Hansen looked like he felt out of place, squeezing into a corner of the booth with his hands folded on the table. Just not his thing, Ditch guessed.

Reynalds was calmly sauntering back from the bar ordering, confidently lighting a cigarette. White was still glancing suspiciously at faded red plaid shirts and John Deere caps. Next to him, Lawrence spoke up, "I'll bet most people in here have never seen a black man in their entire lives." He leaned back and crossed his legs thoughtfully as White shot his glance at him.

"That's not true," Ditch countered, cupping his hands in front of him. "This isn't Hicksville."

"You don't have to get all defensive," Lawrence cut in.

"I'm not being defensive." Ditch looked up at the bar, wondering what the hell was taking so long. Into his field of vision came Holforth, returning from a bathroom stop. Tucking in his Emory T-shirt, Holforth slid into the booth next to Reynalds.

"Well," said Reynalds, grabbing the ashtray and tilting his ash over the black plastic rim, "it's about freakin' time. This like a ritual or something, you have to take a piss first thing in a bar?"

"Hey, man, I just gotta weak bladder, okay?"

"Yeah, but we haven't had more than a beer apiece yet."

Holforth laughed good-naturedly. "When you gotta go, you gotta go, I guess."

Ditch grimaced. White groaned. "Man, that all you can come up with?"

"What?"

"Aw, c'mon, man," White complained, "all you say is 'well, uh, you gotta go, huh huh'..."

"Hey, that was pretty good," Lawrence commented. "Sounded just like him."

"Thanks, Larry," Holforth said, annoyed, as White continued his diatribe. "I mean, you got no creativity, you know what I'm sayin'? Somebody disses you, you give 'em some, you know, something stupid like that? No way, man, you burn 'em good, you know? Somethin' original, you know, like..."

"Like what?"

"I'm coming to it, awright?"

"Yeah, listen to the expert here on comebacks," Reynalds remarked, lazily stubbing out his cigarette and reaching for another. Lawrence laughed. "Fuck you, man!" White said, raising his voice. "You so fucking smart, Mr. Yale, Mr. big fucking rich white college dude..."

Lawrence cut in, "Knock it off, I went to college."

"Yeah, go ahead, Oreo, you on whitey's side, I see it, yeah..."

Holforth started, "Jeez, c'mon guys..."

"Beer's here," Ditch interrupted. They immediately quieted as a short bulky moustached man set two pitchers on the table and stacked five questionably clean glasses in front of the reclining Reynalds. Ditch reached across the table and began to pour as the man set down a single soda. "Somebody got a coke?" he said flatly, barely hiding a smirk. Hansen set down the salt shaker he'd been fiddling with and reached for the glass.

"Thanks," he mumbled, not looking up.

The server returned to the bar. The table remained quiet for a few moments, listening to the clacking of pool balls and subdued talk near the front door. Ditch tilted the first pitcher of Michelob, emptied out a glassful. "Quiet in here, isn't it?" Hansen said haltingly. Reynalds slowly exhaled, "Yeah."

White shifted nervously. "Hey, I thought we gonna see a movie."

"You know, Ditch," Holforth said suddenly, "that was some pitching tonight." He turned around his cap, dirty from the day's play, coughing from Reynalds' smoke. "I mean, you shut them down good."

Ditch leaned forward and crossed his arms on the table. "I'd rather not talk about the game right now."

"Why not?" Hansen asked. "Eric here's been telling me about this pitch you throw, like a slurve or something."

Ditch shook his head and downed his beer. "Just some trick pitch."

"Jesus, Ditch," Holforth said, "what's wrong with you? You always act this mopey?"

"Stop that," White snapped.

Holforth turned. "Huh?"

White reached into his shirt and pulled out a tiny gold crucifix on a chain. "See this?" he asked, face becoming serious. "This here's the man, this here is my savior, Lord Jesus Christ. An' I don't want none of you going 'round taking his name in vain, got it?"

"Give me a fucking break!" Reynalds laughed.

"I mean it, man," said White, shaking the crucifix. "Believe in him and live. I believe it." He nodded as he shook the chain. "You don't gotta believe, I don't care. But don't you go blaspheming 'round me. I don't wanna hear it."

"Okay, okay, calm down, geez."

Lawrence steepled his fingers on the table, and White slowly tucked the cross and chain under his button-up white shirt, carefully rearranging the chain around his neck like tightening a tie. Holforth coughed noisily and reached for the remaining pitcher. "You know," he began, covering his mouth with one hand as he coughed, louder this time, "I read somewhere that second-hand smoke causes something like 50,000 deaths a year."

"That's bullshit," Reynalds snorted, taking a drag and tipping the ashes.

Holforth coughed. "I'm just saying what I read," he answered. "I mean, I don't know..." He coughed again, and wheezed.

"Okay, okay," Reynalds griped, "I'm putting it out." Wisps of light grey smoke curled above the booth from the crushed butt. Reynalds sat back with a huff and crossed his arms. Hansen quietly sipped his coke. Lawrence didn't move, staring dispassionately at his hands in front of him. A moment passed. "I think," Lawrence said lightly, "this is what you might call 'awkward.'"

"Fucking boring is what I'd call it, man," White said, slamming down his glass. The noise startled Ditch, and the table seemed to awaken from a lazy slumber. White pointed a finger at Ditch across the table, exclaiming, "What the fuck do I care if you don't wanna have fun? I mean, what the fuck, man, this all you do? Drink and mope around and shit?"

"Lay off him," Hansen suddenly broke in with an angry tone. White looked at him and was about to reply when Holforth interposed. "Uh, look, I've got an idea." They all looked at him. He coughed, took a swallow from his beer. "I mean, to sort of, uh, get to know each other, we could, y'know, talk about our heroes or something."

Reynalds snorted again. "Give me a break..."

"Will you shut up?" White said. "Man, you worse than Ditch."

"Anyway," Holforth hurriedly continued, "I mean, when I'm behind the plate, I try to pretend I'm, you know, one of the greats sometimes. Like Carlton Fisk or Johnny Bench."

"How about Tim McCarver?" Hansen asked.

"Who?"

"You know, the 'thinking man's catcher.' He caught Steve Carlton."

"Oh." Holforth seemed at a loss. "Well, uh, yeah, I guess so. Carlton was on the Phillies in '80, right?"

"Yeah, he started with the Cards in the late '60s, with Bob Gibson," Hansen replied, sitting up straighter. The baseball talk seemed to energize him. He turned to Ditch. "That before your time, Ditch? You know what I'm talking about?"

"Hey, you don't need my approval," Ditch said, shrugging. "When I was in high school, everybody was talking about Guidry and Valenzuela. I guess Carlton was still around."

"Yeah," Hansen nodded. To Hansen's left, Reynalds sighed, stretching an arm over the booth. "Fernando's coming back, you know. He signed on with the Pods," Hansen added.

"Hey, I didn't know you were this into it," Holforth said.

"Well," Hansen said hesitantly, "I guess I'm kind of a student of the game."

"That's my line!"

"Man, you guys is all stuck in the past," White laughed finally. "No time like the present, know what I'm saying? Look at my man Junior. I read in Sports Illistrated or something where he say he don't know a damn thing about pitchers, he just step up there and hit the ball."

"Damn straight," Lawrence chipped in.

"Hey," Holforth said in White's direction, "if you're a pitcher, how come all your idols are, you know, position guys. Dunston and Junior."

White shrugged. "Dunno, man. I just like 'em, that's all. They play good ball."

"Good enough for me," Ditch said, finishing the last of the beer. "Even after I turned into a pitcher, I still wanted to be like Mike Schmidt."

"So," Lawrence said steadily, "he does talk." White laughed suddenly at the remark. Lawrence looked sideways at White, and flashed a quick grin before glancing back to Ditch. "Why don't you like talking about baseball?"

Ditch shook his head. "I dunno. I just...I don't know, sometimes I feel like if all I do is talk about baseball, pretty soon I won't have anything left to talk about."

Lawrence gazed thoughtfully, and slowly nodded. "I know what you mean. Sometimes, I wonder, 'I have a good college degree, I could get a real job, why am I wasting my time in crappy buses, making near-poverty wages?'"

He paused and shook his head, as if trying to rouse himself. "But then I guess I just like playing the game too much. I guess..."

"Come on, homey," White slapped Lawrence on the shoulder. "That's loser talk, man. You love the game, ain't nothing to be ashamed of."

Ditch sat forward and addressed White bluntly, "You ever feel like you're stuck playing a little kid's game?"

White shook his head emphatically, "No, sir. This here's the greatest game in the world, this here's the greatest job in the world. It ain't about the money, man, it's about the thing. It's about baseball, you know, what makes it a big thing, you know, something that we can relate to, like a...a..."

He searched for a word. "Culturally reinforcing phenomenon?" Lawrence suggested. White stopped. "Sorry," Lawrence smiled, "sociology."

White laughed. "Whatever, man. I don't need your fancy college stuff to know what I'm saying.

"I mean, I know where you're all coming from. I gotta woman back home, two kids already, and I miss 'em. I think of 'em every day we on the road, every time before I start a game, I think of 'em, sitting back home and waiting for me to come back. But..." he paused again, searching, "I can't just stop. It's like, I dunno, I'm part of something, something bigger than just me and my family, you know?"

He sat back, frustrated. "Just forget it. I don't know how to say what I wanna say. Just forget it."

"I know what you mean," Holforth said.

"Yeah?"

"Yeah, I think so. I mean, I gotta girl waiting back home...I mean, I hope she's waiting...and sometimes I think I'm wasting my time playing games." Holforth stopped. "And...?" Hansen prompted. Holforth took his cap off by the bill and tapped the plastic strap at its back on the table's edge. He pursed his lips and frowned. "You know what I read about Carlton Fisk? He said that when he was in the minors, sometimes he felt so lonely, and lost and ready to despair and all that, and that when he went out drinking after weekend games, he'd sit at a bar and pull out pictures of his wife and kid, and he'd sit there with the pictures on the bar, just looking at them, for hours."

Holforth stopped and put his cap back on, the right way this time. He rubbed his hand across his face, pulling his cheeks tight and letting them go. "I think of that sometimes, in the hotel in Buffalo, or Williamsport, or wherever. And then when I step out on the field, it all goes away. The anthem plays over some loudspeaker, the ump shouts play ball, and then nothing else matters. This feeling comes over me, the plate don't seem the way it was in practice, it's like, I don't know, it's like..."

"See?" White said, "I tol' you it ain't easy."

"Yeah."

Lawrence shook his head. "The philosophy of baseball."

Reynalds yawned, mumbling, "You're all romantics."

Holforth glanced at him. "Yeah?"

White reached over and tried to pry open Reynalds' eyes. Reynalds indignantly pushed away White's hands, sputtering. "What the eff are you doing?"

"Don't bark at me, man," White complained. "Thought you was dead."

"Well, maybe I was," Reynalds retorted, rubbing his knuckles into his eyes. "You guys bored me to fucking death. Bunch of idealists."

"So what?" Ditch said. "What's it to you?"

Reynalds reached into his pocket for a cigarette. "Me, I'm a pragmatic." He attempted to light up, and stopped when Holforth began coughing automatically. Annoyed, Reynalds dropped his dollar-fifty lighter to the table and crossed his arms. "Baseball's a job, and I'm good at it."

"Well, well, listen to Mr. Yale going on," White commented.

Reynalds stubbornly continued, "I like being a first baseman, and I'm good at it, and I like being paid for it.

Someday, I'm going to be up there in the majors getting paid even more for it. Megabucks."

Holforth shrugged. "Well, as long as you like it..."

White made a move to get up. "To hell wi' this, man. You guys is so damn negative, I ain't been more bored in my whole life. I'm outta here."

"Hey!" Lawrence yelped. "What do you think you're doing?" White had a foot on the table as he grabbed the booth with one hand. "Getting the hell outta this redneck joint," he said, trying to climb over the half-empty glasses. He steadied himself by placing his hands on Lawrence's head. Holforth alertly rescued the pitcher, and Reynalds opened his eyes quickly enough to avoid White's sneakered feet descending rapidly to the floor.

"Aw, c'mon, man..." Holforth started.

"Fuck you," White said in a spate of anger, snatching his warm-up jacket from one of the bench posts. "Fuck this. I had it with this place. I had it with this town. I had it with you clowns. Ta hell with y'all, I'm gone. Gonna go see a movie or something."

He jerked his arms into the jacket and jaunted out the door, letting a warm summer breeze rush into the air-conditioned bar behind him.

Holforth slowly placed the pitcher back on the table, Reynalds folded his arms again and quietly smirked. Hansen slowly swished the remains of his melted ice and coke with a small circular motion of his wrist. Lawrence rested his elbow on the table, rhythmically tapping a forefinger against his forehead. The clinking of the pool balls briefly dominated the conversation.

"Well," Ditch spoke, "that wasn't too negative, was it?"

He set his glass down and stood. "We can worry about who owes what later." Next to him, Holforth pushed his chair back to let Ditch and Hansen out. "It's about time for the movie to start," Ditch continued. "We'd better catch up to him, he doesn't know his way around. Dave, maybe you oughta talk to him first."

Reynalds let out a belch and then noisily got to his feet. Without looking up, Lawrence said suddenly, "You know what he'll say. He'll say, 'Hey, look like they sent the nigga to talk to the nigga.'"

Holforth began to say something, but Lawrence cut him off angrily. "You all think we're some sort of black club? That all the 'bruthas' hang out with each other or something?"

Ditch spread his hands in a conciliatory gesture. "No, that's not what I mean, c'mon." He sighed. "I just mean, you're his roommate and all, so..."

"Yeah, well, I don't see you hanging out with Hank."

"I don't speak Spanish, he doesn't speak English, I told you…"

"Yeah, yeah." Lawrence rubbed his eyes with his hands and relaxed his shoulders, slowly getting to his feet. "Yeah, yeah, I'll go talk to him. He's probably standing out on the corner, bouncing up and down on his toes talking to himself."

The other five hung back to let Lawrence exit the bar first, then ambled after him. Reynald's first action upon setting foot on the sidewalk was to light the cigarette he had been hiding up his jacket sleeve, letting it drop into his palm then popping it straight upwards without hesitation.

"Neat trick," Holforth commented.

"Thanks," Reynalds replied easily through the side of his mouth, taking a drag.

They stood around with their hands in their pockets, trying to pretend they weren't listening to Lawrence and White conversing on the street corner just a few yards to the right of the bar front. Ditch leaned against a telephone pole. "What movie's starting now?" Hansen asked.

"Dunno. Most of the late movies start right about now."

"So, like, where's the movie theaters around here?"

Ditch considered. "Well, most of them are kinda out of the way. You know, on the outskirts of the city, in the mall. Only takes about fifteen minutes to get there."

"Yeah, but I'm the only one with their car here," Holforth said briefly. "And it don't seat six. So...what else?"

"There's a couple little places a few blocks from here. They show stuff from a few months ago." Still talking in quieter tones, Lawrence and White slowly approached the group. Ditch nodded in their direction. "We were just talking about movies. A couple movies are playing close by, if you wanna go there."

Eyes fixed to the ground, White put his hands in his pockets and scuffed his feet for a moment. "Okay," he said, looking up with a smile, "what you got?"

"Well," Ditch paused, "lessee...I think one place is showing *Major League Two*..."

"Seen it," Hansen interrupted. "It wudn't too good."

"Sucked," said Reynalds.

"...and the other's showing *Henry the Fifth*..."

"The fifth who?" Holforth asked.

"Henry. King of England."

"What the hell's that all about, I thought they had a queen or something."

"Look, Eric," Lawrence interjected, "it's an adaptation of a Shakespearian play. Directed by Kenneth Branagh. Lots of blood and gore, some pretty good acting."

The group began walking as an entity separate from individual thought, each member unconsciously keeping step with each other. Holforth still looked confused. "Shakespearian? Okay, Hamlet, Romeo and Juliet, right?"

"You don't know who Shakespeare was?" Hansen asked surprised.

Reynalds chucked his cigarette into the empty street. "Are you sure you went to college? What was it, Vandy?"

Holforth threw his arms up. "I majored in business, for Chr...okay? I don't know dick about this lit stuff! 'Sides, I didn't even graduate."

"You, too?" Ditch asked.

"Yeah. Cut out early for the draft."

"Maybe we should see *Major League* anyway," Hansen interposed.

"No way," they all shook their heads. "Forget it, man," White said. "You sure we can't go see sumthin inneresting, like, I wanna see *Broken Arrow* or the flick with Coolio and that white chick."

"We got no way to get there," Ditch said. "And we'd get there after they started, probably."

"Look," said Holforth, "I don't feel like seeing some art movie that makes my brain numb, so ain't there something else we can do?"

"Hey, you guys were the ones who wanted to go to the movies..."

Ditch broke off as they approached an intersection. "Check it out." He pointed across to a corner theater sign. Beneath the giant red letters which spelled out "State," the bright white triangular sign stretched over the sidewalk in front of a dark-brown brick building. The outline of mostly lit tiny yellow bulbs highlighted the words in black letters: JUDGE DREDD.

Ditch grinned happily. "We," he announced triumphantly, "are going in there." And he crossed the street without looking, heading straight for the opened red double doors.

"What?" Reynalds protested, following.

"Comic book character, I think," Lawrence said.

"Yeah," Ditch said over his shoulder, entering the theater. "C'mon, check this out."

"Hang on," Hansen chirped, "comic books? How old are you again, 28? 29?" The odor of popcorn pervaded the humid air lingering over the pavement outside the theater. Hansen closed his eyes, sniffing, smiled and followed Ditch into the building. Ditch's voice could be heard sneaking out the doorway, "Trust me, you'll get a kick out of it. It's Stallone."

"*Demolition Man*, right?" Holforth called. He shrugged, stepping onto the faded red carpet. "Good enough for me." Reynalds and Lawrence reluctantly followed suit. "No way, man," White complained, trying to squeeze between Reynalds and Holforth at the soda counter. "My man Wesley Snipes kicked his sorry ass."

12

Restless Monday night in his hotel room after the first of two games in Welland, Ontario, John slowly got up from his bed and softly padded across the floor to the bathroom. His roommate was snoring loudly and mumbling occasionally in his sleep. John flicked on the bathroom light and closed the door, taking a seat on the john to read the baseball book he'd brought with him.

Less than a full page later, he realized that he had read the same paragraph four times already and still had no idea what he had read. His mind wasn't paying attention; the urge to write began to invade the vacant, receptive conscious workings of his frontal lobe. He crept out into the room again, searching for his notebook. Unzipping the duffel bag at the foot of his bed, John rummaged through dirty socks and shorts and felt his fingers touch the warped wire binding of the notebook. He tugged and it came out, dragging behind underwear that it had hooked. Luckily the pen was still trapped within the wire loops.

He stole back into the bathroom and locked the door,

hoping that the overhead ceiling exhaust fan which automatically turned on with the light wasn't loud enough to wake Aguirre. Now that he had a pen in his hand, the unbidden thoughts lay buried again. He searched his recent memory for words, a key phrase that must have set his mind astir. Nothing. John tapped the pen cap against his upper lip. He couldn't remember.

The next best thing was to simply write and hope that whatever it was he knew he wanted to write would somehow mysteriously appear on the pages straddling his naked knees. What if he were to write short descriptions of his teammates? It's what Grant wanted in a column; maybe it would eventually become the next one.

He put pen to paper and jotted down:

Members of the Gladden Fords Wildcats 1995:

Their life and times

After a brief pause, he quickly crossed it out with a crooked x over the entire line and turned to a clean page and tried writing a bit neater.

A few colorful ballplayers who I have been privileged to know.

Hmmm. He tapped the pen against his upper lip, pausing to chew the end of the cap. In parentheses underneath the title he added in careful script:

(or, what lunatics are among us)

The pen raised its blue tip for a second, as he thought about how utterly inane he was being, but as he knew no one would ever see what he was writing unless he rewrote it all anyway, he allowed the pen to continue.

According to the original "introductory" column by Mike Grant, friend and aspiring humorist, this team is the "best crop of young talent" in all of New York. I don't think he was including the Mets and Yankees, but you never know.

I don't know more than a handful of the players, since I tend to keep to myself most of the time. No, wait, this is too conversational, maybe I should just list their names and hometowns and all that.

He stopped again and reread what he had just written. His thoughts were transfixing him; abruptly he ignored it all and kept writing.

Paul Hansen. Last year's USA Today runner-up high school all-America baseball MVP (courtesy of Mike's article). They'd call it "second team," like in most high school and college conferences, but I guess they thought "runner-up" didn't sound as bad as "second best." He's about 6'2", kind of on the skinny side though I think he could put on some muscle and weight in a few years. Listens to industrial music, warms in the bullpen to Nine Inch Nails. Pretty smart for a guy who decided to skip college entirely. I don't know about book smart. Guess there's a difference between intelligent and smart. Throws lefty, lots of heat and tricky slider. Rumors are that he's bound for the majors in two years, three tops. Should be, with the money he's already getting. I'm jealous as hell.

Rick Reynalds. From Conn. Big guy, about 6'4" and

probably pushing 220, maybe more. Fields like a cement block and sometimes acts like one. I wonder if he knows he's antagonizing everyone, maybe he does it on purpose. Talks endlessly about money. Doesn't really act like an ivy leaguer. Right-handed, not an advantage for a first baseman. He should be able to pound the ball, I think he's trying to hit five-run homers all the time.

Hank Aguirre. My own roommate. I think he's from Arizona or New Mexico, either an immigrant or first-generation. I can barely understand his English, but he probably can't understand me either. We don't talk too much, when we're on the road he usually hangs out with the guys who can speak Spanish. Eric can, sort of, but says he feels uncomfortable with them. Hank seems obsessed with card games. Other than that, he's a reliever with heat and that's all I know.

Dave Lawrence. We call him Larry most of the time, a good starter, went to University Illinois Urbana-Champaign. Talks and sometimes acts the smooth cat. From South Side Chicago, I think. Cool accent, wish I could do it. I tried to talk like that, but it just sounds unnatural and fakey, so I stopped trying. He's around 6 feet and 180 or so, wide-receiver size for football. Throws mostly fastball and works on his overhand curve too much. Probably our best starter, good instincts, especially fielding.

Shawon White. I asked him once if he was related to Roy White and he just looked at me like he'd never heard the name before. From Mississippi, close to Louisiana border, talks about his wife and two kids a lot. I hope they're still waiting for him. About 5'10", second shortest pitcher, next to me. 170 probably. On the slender side, but pretty strong. Throws almost 95, but needs control and another pitch. No change, slider's flat. Gets mad real easy. He's blown a lead twice already, lost one game because he lost his temper at himself and almost lost another. Eric says he's sick of having to calm him down, because when he gets mad he talks to himself out loud on the mound and ignores everything else. I don't know about his religion. Swears an awful lot, likes sex jokes sometimes racial jokes, but gets mad whenever anyone says Jesus or God without praying for real. Likes to stay up late. I wonder how long he'll last.

Eric Holforth. Basically my best friend on the team, if I had a best friend. Built like a tank, got an arm like a cannon. An even 6 feet, I think, maybe a half inch shorter, but he'd never admit that. Left Vanderbilt early, says he shouldn't have gotten in there anyway because he never did any work but got away with it for almost three years. I wonder if his scholarship was about to run out or be taken away and that's why he jumped. Technically not too smart, but he calls a better game than almost anyone I've ever seen, knows where everything's at on the field, takes charge without being a total asshole about it. He's still like a big teenager, but on the field everyone listens to him, including coaches. Real easy-going, hard to piss off.

Eduardo Corrales. Supposed to be our star third baseman, says Mike. Real good fielder, haven't seen him hit much yet. Then again, neither has anybody in the league yet. Don't know too much else about him. Looks all of 16 or 17. Think he's from Nicaragua.

Bill Collins. The manager from hell...

The pen lifted and hovered above the notebook for a while as John's mind came up blank. While his mind focused in and out of itself the pen took the opportunity to retrace several random words, making them much more difficult to read. He haphazardly underlined a few names, but decided he didn't like the way it looked. Taking the cap out from between his teeth, John swiped two lines underneath the bottom line of the text, dated it, and closed the notebook up again. He didn't have his watch on, so he couldn't tell for sure what time it was, but it felt like he had been sitting in the bathroom for half an hour or so. The light turned off and the door gently unlocked, John stumbled into the dark and groped his way along the foot of the bed to his duffel bag. The bedside LCD clock claimed he'd been writing for over an hour; he supposed it was possible. He always lost track of time while writing.

The next morning he'd have to look over what he had written. Maybe make a column out of it. He lay back in bed and listened to the distant rumble of rigs on the QEW and the roar of Niagara Falls.

13

Fans had already begun to pack into the ballpark in Batavia for the one o'clock Wednesday businessman's lunch game between the Clippers and the Wildcats. On the field, it was the Wildcats' turn to take batting practice; Lawrence, since it was his second day after starting a game, was throwing lolly-pops to the batters, while Hansen, who had started the previous day in Elmira, stood guard behind the pitchers warming up along the sidelines. The Clippers were still preparing for their infield and batting practice, but their starting pitcher was just finishing his warm-ups along the right field wall. A few Clippers autographed the hats and white program guides of seven and eight-year-old fans who crowded along the fence next to the dugout.

Stretching out his legs near the left field wall, Ditch touched his fingertips to his toes, feeling the knots in his lower back complain. He held the position for a few moments, then relaxed and moved his head clockwise in a circle to try to undo the knots in his neck. The rhythmic thwacking of the batting practice balls and the thudding of the pitched balls into catchers' mitts was conspiring with the afternoon warmth and humidity to make him feel slightly buzzed. He decided he'd better get up and head to the outfield for a few wind sprints.

As he stood and cracked his back, Ditch heard someone from his right call his name. The pitching coach Kriek was approaching from the dugout, hands in jacket pockets, pudgy aged face chewing at something. He stretched his right arm over his head while waiting for the coach to near. The coach briefly looked out at the field, then at Ditch. "After these guys here get done with their pitches," he said slowly through the chewing of the gum-like substance. Motioned to the two relievers throwing on the sideline bullpen mounds. "Mr. Collins wants you to throw some, about 20, 30 pitches."

Ditch paused, his right arm still stretched above his head. "Coach," he began, "you know how many innings I've pitched already this week?"

There was no response from the older man, who methodically chewed whatever it was he had in his mouth. Ditch continued, "Let's see, today's June 30th. We've played, what, 12 games, including today, and I've pitched in 9 of them. My arm's beat."

Kriek spat a huge gob of something at the base of the wall. "I'm just telling you what Mr. Collins said."

"Yeah, well, when I came in last night to face two batters, he told me I wouldn't have to pitch today."

Kriek said nothing. He wouldn't even look at Ditch, instead pretending to study the motion and delivery of one of the young pitchers warming in the pen. The other pitchers, already seated in gray metal chairs against the wall, were trying very hard not to appear as if they were overhearing the conversation.

"All right," Ditch said after a few seconds, "maybe if my arm falls off, he won't be able to pitch me tomorrow. My arm gets any more tender, you can chop it off and serve it as veal cutlet." He picked up his glove from his chair and jogged to left field to do his wind sprints. Reaching the left-center field alley, he turned back to see Kriek picking up a mitt, as the catchers needed to take turns in the batting cage. In a few minutes the day's starting pitcher, White, would come out of the dugout and throw a couple dozen warm-up pitches as the Wildcats' infield would take their turn warming up on the field before the game would begin. A batted ball landed a few yards in front of him, hitting the short grass and bounding towards the wall. A youthful outfielder came running over to scoop up the ball, not wasting a look at him, and flung it towards the back-up infielder stationed midfield. Ditch waited until a lefty stepped into the batter's box, and, gripping his glove's folded fingers in his left hand, he sprinted back and forth between center and left field six times before finally returning to the now vacant bullpen.

Upon his return to the pen, Ditch took a few minutes to mop his brow with the faded blue-striped towel which adorned his chair, and then he took a shot of water from his squeeze bottle, swishing the water around his mouth before spitting it out on the nearest mound. The bullpen catcher, Stanley, tossed him a ball, and he bent his head to the task of digging a small trench next to the rubber with his right heel. He looked up at the sound of the loudspeaker announcing the start of the game. As his name was called, each Clipper player ran out to his position on the field and began to pound his glove. The last name announced belonged to the opposing pitcher, who was already on the mound taking his allotted ten pitches while the position players behind him briefly threw a ball around the horn. The Wildcats leadoff batter was announced, and as he stepped in and waved his bat somewhat frenetically, Ditch placed his right foot into the trench and began lobbing throws to Stanley, making giant circles with his pitching arm after each throw, as if he were winding an enormous clock. Mr. Collins, he noted sardonically, had not specified the speed of his "20 or 30 pitches."

The first inning went by quickly for both sides, all six

batters being set down without incident. Stopping at a baker's dozen, Ditch finished his pitches during the top of the second, and so was able to watch the Wildcats put two men on base, one by walk, the other by error, with only one out. A mild summer breeze had picked up a bit, blowing in from the northwest off Lake Ontario and cutting across from left to right field. The businessman's lunch crowd at the park cheered as the Wildcats batter popped the ball up to short center, and then quieted as the Clippers' center fielder misjudged the wind-swept ball, diving at the last second and missing it to his left. The scoreboard registered it as a single, and the Wildcats had the first run of the game, runners still on first and second. Ditch fetched a ziplock bag full of sunflower seeds out of his duffel bag and passed it down the line of relievers. They set up a used water cup roughly ten feet away from the center of the line of chairs and took turns flicking shells towards it as the half inning dragged on.

The starter for the Clippers was eventually yanked after the Wildcats had piled up five runs, mostly on walks and miscommunication among the Clipper infielders. As the opposing pitcher trudged with head down toward his dugout to a mixture of cheers and catcalls from the crowd, Ditch couldn't help feeling a brief stab of sympathy. It had happened to him plenty of times before; sometimes, no matter how well a pitcher was throwing, a string of lucky breaks for the other team was all it took. He grunted, stretched his arms, fingers locked in front of him, and absent-mindedly surveyed the shell-shucked pen as the relievers took a timeout from their sport. On the field, the Clippers' manager had brought in a right-handed reliever to face a lefty batter, which probably meant that the Clippers either didn't have a lefty reliever, or that their lefty was too tired to pitch today. Ditch hoped his manager had noticed that.

Three batters later the first reliever left, having gotten exactly zero batters out. Eleven Wildcat batters had been at the plate so far, and now Reynalds stepped in with the bases loaded and seven runs in. Ditch checked the sunflower supply; it was running low already, but at least one more reliever had brought his own supply, so there would be enough for probably two, three innings, if they stretched them out. Despite the breeze, it was getting hot and muggy down on the field. One of the relievers disappeared into the dugout and returned with an armful of dampened towels. Even with a towel draped over his head and covering his ears, Ditch could still hear a few hometown fans behind him in the bleachers shouting at their pitcher "You suck!" and "Get this loser the hell outta here!"

Reynalds quickly ended the inning by grounding into a 4-6-3 double play. The Clippers ran in from the field, the Wildcats ran out, bringing gloves and hats for the former base runners. Reynalds stood on first base, angrily peeling off his batting gloves. He made a motion to throw his helmet but instead restrained himself by handing it to a batboy. Tossing his gloves into the helmet, he caught his hat and glove from the passing right fielder and immediately threw the ball on the ground to the third baseman. Ditch grabbed the now almost-dry towel from his head, tugged his hat on and trekked in to the dugout for a visit with the orange water cooler, a trip he suspected he would make many more times before the afternoon was through.

Once back in the pen, he slouched in his seat, draping his arms over the two empty chairs to either side of him and gazed wearily out at the field from underneath the shade of the refreshed towel. The bottom of the second had begun, and White continued to look good, blowing the first two pitches right past the Clippers cleanup batter. On the third pitch, a waste pitch low and outside, White took extra time walking around the mound, circling in a stilted manner. He threw another pitch, another wasted pitch, but it traveled farther outside than the catcher expected, as the ball barely grazed the edge of Holforth's outstretched mitt. From his seat in the pen, Ditch could see Holforth throw a new ball to White while motioning with his mitt for the pitcher to calm down. Another pitch zipped across the plate outside of the strike zone, but this time the batter swung mightily and hit it off the end of his bat. The ball slowly rolled between first base and the pitcher's mound; White charged it and pegged a bare-handed throw at the second baseman who was trying to backup an indecisive Reynalds at first. The throw went wild, and Reynalds almost collided into the runner by reaching across the base path with his glove hand for the ball. The second baseman kept after the ball, which luckily rebounded sharply backwards from the right field wall and prevented the runner from heading towards second. White lay flat on his back, holding his right leg as the trainer and pitching coach rushed out from the dugout.

As the two coaches made White put his arms around their shoulders, Ditch guessed what had happened: during the lengthy half inning in which the Wildcats batted around, White had forgotten to stretch out. His muscles had begun to tighten in the heat of the day and he had pulled a hamstring or groin muscle, probably at least a two week injury, maybe more. And now someone would have to warm up and go in for a few innings to hold the lead until the setup man could come in around the 6th or 7th.

"Klein!" Collins hollered down the line. He had emerged and was walking out onto the field towards his injured pitcher. He waved for Ditch to come on and pitch.

At first Ditch couldn't respond. He sat on his chair,

arms still draped over the backs of the adjacent chairs. After a long moment, he pursed his lips and spat the seed he'd been chewing on towards the cup, watching the tiny ripped shell flutter a few feet and disappear into the grass without a sound. Picking up his hat and glove as deliberately as possible, Ditch removed the towel and carefully walked to the mound, making sure to step on third base on the way there. He wasn't particularly superstitious, but his roommate Hank was and was sure to give him a hard time if he didn't follow the correct procedure. Besides, he figured it couldn't do any harm.

The loudspeaker in the park came on with a small bit about a contest in the day's program. Holforth was waiting at the mound holding his mask and catching helmet in his mitt. As they talked, the two watched the coaches gingerly guide White into the shade of the dugout and towards the locker room beyond.

"Surprised to see you out here again," Holforth said.

"Yeah, right." Ditch began digging the trench in front of the rubber a bit deeper. "Lemme tell you straight up: my arm's dead. Totally. I need about three days off, it's so dead."

"Okay, then I'll call for the pitch a lot."

Ditch looked up.

"Don't gimme that," Holforth replied to the look. "See, it's kinda windy right now, and the pitch is kinda like a sinker ball. You pitch three-quarters anyway..."

"Yeah, okay, and when sinker ballers get tired, the more tired they get, the further the ball drops, right?"

"Now you're with the program," Holforth said, hitting Ditch in the left shoulder with a mock fist. The infielders who had been gathered in a crowd between first and second had moved over to behind the mound. Reynalds stubbornly remained at first base, pounding his glove, as if he needed to guard the runner during an injury time out. Holforth motioned for him to join the group. Examining the stitching of his glove, Reynalds wandered towards the mound.

"Okay, here's what's happening," Holforth addressed the group, standing with his back to the plate and holding his mitt up to cover his mouth from any would-be lip readers in the Clippers dugout. "Hold your gloves up so they don't know if we're all talking or not," Holforth instructed, which they all did. "We're gonna give these guys a steady diet of sinkers, so they're gonna be pulling it on the ground and hitting it the other way if they pop it up. The next two guys are righties, so that means you," he pointed at the third baseman Corrales, who nodded slightly and softly pounded his glove. One by one they split off and returned to their positions.

Reynalds had the batboy retrieve the infielder's ball and began making the rounds again. The catcher returned to behind the plate, and Ditch signed with his glove the desired warm-up pitches.

The glove went out straight twice in a row, two fastballs. Then out and back, change up. Finally, in a circle, curve ball. After only the fourth pitch, Ditch held his hand up to signal he was done. Holforth came out to talk again while behind him the home umpire had turned his rear towards the field and was briskly sweeping the plate.

"You sure you're ready? You get all the pitches you want, you know."

Pretending to work on the trench again, Ditch only nodded.

"Right. First pitch'll be a straight fastball, inside corner, high. Then we go from there." Holforth returned to the plate, and the inning began again.

Two pitches later, Ditch was resting in the dugout, a towel over his head once more. A pop out to second and a double-play grounder to third: Holforth had correctly guessed first-pitch swinging and gotten good location without making his pitcher throw a sinker yet. Ditch mopped his face as he watched the Wildcats go down quietly in their half of the third. He knew he would pitch at least through the third, possibly the fourth...Collins had yet to talk to him since calling on him to replace White. Quickly he tried to banish all thoughts of fatigue from his mind; tired as he knew he was, he'd just have to take it one batter at a time and let Collins do the managing.

After two more innings, however, he found himself wondering how long he actually would stay in. The third had gone fairly easily, and the fourth, though he allowed a bloop double, wasn't exactly hard work, but he could feel that any speed he had on his fastball was now gone. That also meant the change was no good, because it wasn't changing from anything. Collins had made no movement towards even having someone up and throwing in the pen, so Ditch knew he'd pitch the fifth. Now, he supposed, was the time to put Holforth's theory to the test and hope that his quasi-sinker would make up for the missing fastball.

As the bottom of the fifth began, he told Holforth as much, but the catcher reassured him that it would work. They'd only thrown the sinker-slurve twice so far, and then only to lefties so that it might look more like a mistake of a curve on the outside corner. "Just aim for my glove and let the motion take care of itself," Holforth said in a mini-conference at the mound.

"What if the motion takes itself 50 feet into the ground?"

"Then I'll stop it," Holforth asserted confidently.

They started off the first right-handed batter with a slow curve, which he promptly fouled over the left field wall. The remaining crowd, thinned out after the businessmen had left, gave a big but disappointed cheer as the ball disappeared from sight. The catcher called time and jogged out to the mound with a new ball. "Right, now we make it look like I'm concerned you're getting tired," he said tonelessly, covering up his speech with the mitt. He glanced at the dugout, in case Collins had started to pay attention, Ditch assumed. He nodded his head as glumly as possible and dug at his trench. Holforth handed him the ball and patted him on the shoulder before retreating.

The crowd made some noise as the batter readied in the box, but quieted as the batter swung ahead of and over the pitch: sinker, low and inside. Ditch kept his face as stony as he could, and wasted no time pacing about the mound. The next pitch Holforth wanted high and tight, his out-of-gas fastball. The batter stood firm, keeping the bat on his shoulders as he angled his upper body back from the pitch. The next pitch was a sinker low and outside: he weakly tapped it back to the mound, and Ditch took great pleasure in nonchalantly tossing it to first. One down in the fifth, two to go, he thought.

Ditch realized that he now should be working through batters he'd already faced. *Hopefully*, he thought, *I can fool all of them*. But a pinch hitter stepped in, a tall lefty with his socks hiked halfway up his shins. Ditch got the sign from Holforth, who he knew must be making the typical remark about being ready for the next Flood to the batter. They started him with a curve outside, but he didn't bite and it was too high. Ball one. The catcher signaled for another curve; this time the ump gave him the corner. One and one. Now, the first sinker, again outside. Ditch watched it flutter to the right, then dive back towards the outside corner of the plate. Holforth held it intently for a second, but the ump refused to give them the call. Two and one. Holforth wanted another sinker outside. Going into his windup, Ditch knew a split second after he released the ball that he'd put too much on it. The ball crossed the plate low and inside, and the next thing he knew he was watching it fly over the right field fence. The crowd stood and cheered, and the batter rounded the bases as the score board flashed electronic fireworks.

In a flash Holforth was at the mound, saying, "Don't worry about it. He hit a mistake. We're still up by six, don't worry about. Shake it off."

Ditch swore. "Dammit! Low and inside to righties, high and tight to lefties!"

Holforth looked at the batter rounding third and saw the Wildcats third baseman approaching, appearing as if he wanted to add something. Ditch turned around as Corrales nudged him with his glove. "Yeah?"

Corrales spoke in rapid-fire Spanish.

"Sorry, no habla espanol. What'd he say, Eric?"

"Um...lessee..he says your sister's a good ride..."

The third baseman laughed and smacked Holforth with his glove, saying something else. "Oh," Holforth added, "he also says not to worry, just make them hit it at him. At least, I think that's the gist of what he means."

Corrales nodded and stuck out a fist at Ditch, waist-level. Ditch likewise made a fist and the two exchanged light hits on top of the other's fist as Corrales said in his best English, "Go get em keed." He tugged his cap down farther than it already was and trotted back to his position. Holforth imitated the exchange, saying, "Go after them," before returning to his squat behind the plate.

It wasn't easy. The Clippers pinch hit another lefty, and in his effort not to give the batter a good pitch, Ditch wound up issuing a walk on five pitches. Fortunately, the

Clippers seemed to have run out of lefties on the bench, and the subsequent right-handed batter got on top of the second pitch and bounced one to second base for a routine double play. Slowly walking into the dugout, Ditch tried to glance surreptitiously at Collins, who had been standing in his suit near the bat rack the entire game, mesmerizing himself with his charts. Collins didn't even look up. Ditch had to wonder if Collins was actually running the club or if he had decided beforehand to let his coaches make all the decisions. But that would mean that Kriek had made the decision to put him in so early, and as little as he knew about the pitching coach, he knew that Kriek had been uncomfortable earlier telling him to throw.

Maybe Bill's got everything figured out ahead of time, he pondered. *He's got a different command for every situation, like a computer.* Yes, he decided, yes, that was it. The computer model fit Collins perfectly. Ditch sat on the bench on the opposite end from the bat rack and concentrated on the game. He had no clue at all how long he would stay in the game; there was no use in worrying about it, he knew, because in the end the decision would not be up to him anyway. He might just as well get down to pitching and hope that the strain of pitching his strange sinker didn't permanently screw up his already tired arm.

The sixth inning seemed to drag on forever, though according to the clock on the scoreboard it had only taken a little over fifteen minutes. The Wildcats had seen a short rally fail, as they had runners at first and second from two infield singles but couldn't get either in. In the bottom half of the inning, Ditch let in his second run, although it was unearned, when a batter reached on a two-base throwing error by the shortstop, stole third, and then scored on a fly ball. He finally recorded a strikeout, too, getting a burly designated hitter to swing at a slider in the dirt in front of the plate. The inning ended with two men on. Ditch sat next to Holforth this time, hoping they could come up with a plan to make it through the next inning, since there was still no one else warming up to come in for the seventh.

"No way can you go out there again," Holforth said, shaking his head. "No way. Send in Hank, or McBride, anybody."

Ditch shrugged. "No use in me saying anything about it. He's already got me pegged as a chronic complainer." He paused. "...which I guess I am." He rose to get a cup of water and Holforth went to talk to Collins. At the water cooler, Ditch slowly sipped about half the water in his cup before dumping the rest over his head. Holforth and Collins apparently were engaged in an argument at the far end of the dugout. Ditch held a towel under the cooler tap for a few seconds, then wrapped the towel around his neck. At this rate, he figured the three or four coolers the team had in the dugout would be empty by the end of the seventh. Stepping around the cleated feet of position players lounging on the bench, most of them draped with damp towels to combat the rising mid-afternoon heat, he carefully walked back to where Holforth was removing his equipment. The catcher was due to bat sixth in the inning, if they got that far, so he would leave his shin guards on in case he would have to go back onto the field before he batted.

"So," Ditch asked him, "what'd Bill have to say?"

Holforth was silent for a moment, retying one of his shoes. He straightened. "Not much. I told him what I thought, and he thanked me for my opinion."

"So he told you off, then."

"Yeah. He's got ears like a dog, you know." Collins stood at his spot near the bat rack, arms crossed and back ramrod straight. Even in the heat he insisted upon wearing his fedora.

Ditch shrugged and lay back against the cement dugout wall. "I don't care anymore. What's he gonna do, change his mind and not pitch me? I still get paid the same, he doesn't pay my salary."

Holforth made no response to that, watching Corrales line a single to right. A slow moving ground ball to first sent him to second on a fielder's choice, and the third man of the inning walked to make it first and second with one out. Holforth rose to get his bat and helmet. Although technically he was "in the hole," and wasn't allowed in the on deck circle with the batter who was ahead of him, he generally did it anyway. A couple times already that season he'd been ordered by the home plate umpire to go back into the dugout and wait his turn. To play it safe, he stayed behind the circle, but outside the dugout, just a few feet in front of the batting rack.

From his perspective, Ditch could see Holforth down on one knee, propping up one arm with the right knee and half-swinging the bat to practice "breaking" his wrists. Ditch could see his mouth opening, as if he were talking to someone, Collins, most likely. The batter grounded to second, and both runners advanced. Likewise, Holforth advanced to the on deck circle, turning his head to give Collins a parting shot of sorts. The manager immediately snapped his head and barked into the dugout for the backup catcher Stanley, who had been lounging out in the bullpen with the relievers. One of the coaches ran to get Stanley, and Holforth flung his bat at the ground and began shouting at the top of his lungs at his manager. Both umpires called time out as the catcher and manager hurled epithets at each other, both enunciating clearly and loudly enough for most the crowd to hear. At first sign of a war of words, the stands had begun to buzz with anticipation, but now that the two were really starting to go at it, the laughter was building. The crowd was clearly enjoying seeing the visiting players make fools of themselves.

The batting coach had to hold back Holforth from his own manager, and the plate umpire summarily thumbed the catcher out of the game, although evidently he had already been taken out of the game anyway. The crowd gave an enormous cackling cheer as the umpire proceeded to issue a stern warning to a red-faced Collins, which only made the manager more red-faced. But, for the moment, Collins made no reply to the umpire's admonishment. *You always have to draw the line someplace,* Ditch thought, watching Holforth stalk off to the showers. He stuck out a fist as the catcher passed and received a heavy-handed blow in return. Holforth said nothing as he reared back and tossed his helmet onto the field of play near the third base coach's box. The crowd erupted with a roar as the umpire behind second base marched straight over to the dugout and proclaimed a fine of one hundred dollars. Holforth responded by quickly unbuckling his shin guards and tossing them onto the field one after the other. The ump visibly restrained himself as he declared two more fines of a hundred apiece. The crowd noise grew louder and louder with each proclamation.

Despite himself, Ditch grinned. He hadn't known Holforth had a temper this vicious. *If this be treason...he* thought, looking down the dugout at Collins. The manager had rolled up a newspaper and was slowly hitting it against his palm. He darted an ugly look in Ditch's direction and then focused his anger at the field. *You have to draw the line somewhere*, Ditch thought again, realizing this meant Collins would keep him in until his arm quite literally tore itself off...*and sometimes, you get pushed over.*

Stanley predictably struck out swinging on three pitches, each one higher than the previous, as the opposing pitcher "climbed the ladder." The crowd of about a thousand went berserk, the fans behind the Wildcats' dugout banging their fists against the dugout roof. Ditch retrieved his cap and bounded up the steps, making it obvious he wasn't bothering to look at either his pitching coach or manager. Stanley placed his bat and helmet carefully down in the ondeck circle and began the process of assembling his catching gear. Halfway to the mound, Ditch glanced back and saw Collins saying a few things to Stanley. *What else can Bill do?* Ditch wondered, stopping between the plate and the mound to pick up the ball. He tucked his glove under an arm and massaged the leather, seeking out the soft spots to exploit.

Stanley approached the plate, his mitt under one arm as he adjusted the head strap on his face mask. Ditch decided to cut to the chase.

"Look, Frank, lemme tell you straight up, I got no speed on my fastball any more. The last two innings, Eric and I used it to move people off the plate so I could throw sinkers down out of the strike zone."

Stanley paused to take his chewing gum out of his mouth and stick it on the back of his helmet. He nodded, said, "Okay," and put the helmet on and the face mask over it. Ditch nodded back and went to the mound to take his ten pitches.

The first batter stepped in, and Stanley looked to the dugout, signing for a fastball letter high. Ditch nodded. He would go with this one. The ball rose on him a little bit, and Stanley, who was unused to catching with a batter and was also not as quick as Holforth, simply waved his mitt at the pitch as it sailed over his head and slammed into the wooden wall behind the home plate area with a resounding thud. The catcher got to his feet to retrieve the ball, and the crowd cheered loudly again.

Ditch got the ball back and silently dug at his trench. Pounding his mitt once or twice, Stanley looked back into the dugout and gave the sign for a fastball outside and low. Ditch shook it off; Stanley pounded his glove again nervously and gave the sign again. Ditch shook it off again and stepped off. The batter stepped out of the box, the umpire called time, and Stanley pounded his glove, looking into the dugout.

Ditch waved his glove for Stanley to join him at the mound. The catcher jogged up, leaving his mask on.

"Look, Frank," Ditch said before the catcher could say anything. "It's real obvious you're getting the signs from Bill. You have to know that there's no way I can throw two fastballs in a row unless they're both chin music. I'd get killed."

"Yeah." Stanley nodded. He lowered his head and pounded his mitt some more.

Raising his glove to hide his speech from his own dugout, Ditch continued, "I don't want to put you in Bill's doghouse, so I'll take all the blame for this, okay?"

Stanley nodded.

"Here's what we're gonna do. Gimme all the signs, slowly, one after the other, and I'll nod at the pitch I want. Then gimme the location, and I'll nod if I agree with you. And to start off on a good note, the next pitch to this guy's gonna be a curve down the middle. They know something's wrong, so they've probably been told to take everything unless it's a slow fat one. My fastball's big and fat now, so we'll use it to push people away from the plate. Right?"

Stanley nodded, seeming relieved, and returned to the plate. Ditch stared in. He received no signs, so he flipped his glove and brushed the dirt in front of the rubber with one foot, hoping Stanley would at least try to play along with it. The catcher rocked forward onto his knees, looked into the dugout, and then settled back to give a sign: curve. Ditch nodded. The catcher's hand went back towards his crotch: down the middle. Again Ditch nodded. Stanley was catching on.

The pitch curved in at the waist and landed in the catcher's mitt at the knees. A strike. The batter watched it all the way in, released the bat from his shoulder and stepped out for a moment to take a swing or two. *All bets are off*, Ditch thought. *They need baserunners, but the take sign's off*. He stopped Stanley's signs at the slider, and nodded at down, slightly off the middle. *Good*. Stanley was catching on faster than Ditch thought he would. The batter swung over the top of the pitch and bounced it to first for an easy out. Reynalds tossed it around the horn, and as Ditch waited for the ball to return to him, he finally took a look at Collins. The manager was looking incensed as he made a motion for the catcher to speak with him near the on deck circle. Ditch saw Stanley lope over and raise his arms, as if he were saying the pitcher was ignoring him. Ditch smiled. The time was rapidly approaching for the line to be crossed.

Once again behind the plate, Stanley brushed away the dirt from home and made a circle in the air with one finger. Ditch nodded and swept away imaginary dirt from in front of him with a foot. Another righty stepped up to bat, and Stanley looked into the dugout. He signaled for a fastball, then a change, then paused and signed for a sinker. Ditch nodded, and agreed with low and inside. The pitch came straight at the batter's behind, and the batter, retreating in panic, swung awkwardly in defense as the ball crossed over the plate near the inside corner around knee-high. Ditch doubted the pitch would have been called a strike, but it had the desired effect.

Collins came storming out of the dugout and demanded time from the ump. Not bothering to hear if he had gotten it, Collins proceeded to the mound to confront his errant pitcher. Ditch regarded his manager calmly.

"When I give you a sign, mister, I expect you to obey it, you hear?" Collins shouted at him. To Ditch it appeared as if every vein in Collins' face and neck were standing out, giving the manager a curious bright red and blue spider web-like appearance.

"In professional baseball," he replied without a trace

of sarcasm, "it is customary to inform a pitcher ahead of time whether or not he will be allowed to call his own game."

Collins blustered. "My policy has always been..."

"If you have a policy of telling your pitchers to throw big fat ones right down the middle, it's the first I heard of it."

"What!" Collins shouted even louder. "Are you trying to tell me how to run my club?"

The home plate umpire had come halfway up the runway between home and the mound. He was forced to shout because of the increasing crowd noise. "Mr. Collins, I don't recall giving you permission to talk to your pitcher. Either take your pitcher out or return to your team's dugout."

"Shut up, walrus, this is none of your business," Collins hollered at the man in blue. The stands began shaking from the pounding of a thousand pairs of feet. Sensing a climax was near, Ditch wandered towards the plate, where the bemused batter stood resting on his bat.

"Mr. Collins," the ump boomed in a louder voice, "I already warned you once. I do not intend to warn you a second time."

"Well, you just did, didn't you?" Collins shouted back, taking his hat off and gesturing with it. Ditch was too far away now to hear exactly what was being said, but whatever it was, he doubted it was civil. The other umpire had walked over to help his partner, and the batting and pitching coaches of the Wildcats had rushed onto the field to try to calm their manager. The stands were practically tearing themselves up from their flimsy foundations.

Ditch grabbed the batter and shouted at his ear, "Start a fight with me."

"What?" the batsman shouted back.

"Start a fight. Some wrestling, nothing dangerous. Buy you and your friends a round after the game."

"Make it two rounds, and meet us on the field."

"Deal." Ditch promptly shoved the batter to the ground and pounced on him. Both benches turbocharged into action, sweeping up the already arguing participants on the field like a tidal wave crashing down towards an unguarded beachhead. Fans showered debris on top of the mass of tangled bodies, boxes of popcorn, half-drunk plastic glasses of light beer and overpriced half-eaten hotdogs mixing with the swirling sea of light gray and dark red pinstriped uniforms. One of the fans ran onto the field and tried to grab Collins' hat as a battle souvenir but was quickly caught up by the incoming tide.

When it was all over, half a dozen players and two exuberant fans were ejected, along with an irate-beyond-words Collins. A random Clippers coach was likewise ejected, though Ditch suspected it likely that that was to ensure somewhat even distribution of guilt. He, of course, was ejected, as was the batter. It could have been his imagination, but he thought the crowd cheered loudest when Collins' name was mentioned over the loudspeakers. Kriek was tabbed as the acting manager, and the pitching coach immediately installed Ditch's roommate, Aguirre, on the mound. Ditch gathered up his things, bade farewell to his fellow relievers, and left them the remainder of his bag of sunflower seeds as he departed whistling for the showers.

14

Lying on his hotel bed, his roommate already asleep on the other bed, John, though slightly tipsy, decided to write. He turned on the table lamp between the beds to its lowest setting. Aguirre mumbled something inarticulate and rolled over, but did not wake. John quietly found his notebook in his duffel bag at the foot of the bed, and, lying back as softly as possible, he began to write a letter to his manager, beginning,

Dear Bill,

John paused, and then hurriedly wrote down his thoughts as they occurred to him, without editing.

Dear Bill,

That's actually kind of a dumb thing to write, since I'm

not going to write you a letter I'm just sort of practicing for when you call me into your little office and bawl me out for starting a riot. By the time I talk to you in private (or get talked to, more like it) I'll probably forget everything I wanted to say and wind up sounding like a complete moron again, so even though it sounds kind of awkward and it's not exactly authentic, I'm going to write down what I want to say and then try to practice it for later. So here goes.

You are a bad manager. A terrible, wretched excuse for a manager. Of course, I doubt I'll say that to your face, but it's what I think and I think everyone else on the club including your coaches all think this about you. I don't know why you think you have to prove yourself to us by acting like such a complete shit head to your own team. You must be really insecure. I wonder if you hate yourself.

You sure do hate me. Well, at least you take an extreme disliking to me, although I don't know if dislike is a strong enough word for it. You're only 35 but you always try to act like you're a lot older than that, maybe as old as my dad. Are you trying to act like you're a dad to us? Maybe that's why I don't like you at all, because you remind me of my dad too much, the way you always try to have power over me and tell me what I should be doing at every second during the games.

No, that's not it. My dad doesn't do that. He never told me what to do or how to do it, he just made sure I could do what I wanted to do and helped me if he could. He gave me a choice, and I did what I wanted, I did the rest. I think. I don't know any more. All I know is that you're pissing me off and making me want to hate you and hate baseball and hate my family and my job and my life, and for that I hate you.

I wonder if Vi would call this "misplaced anger" or aggression, or whatever the term is. I never could figure out all those psychological terms, all that Freud stuff. I think it's mostly self-masturbation.

But I do know that you won't give me a fair shot at anything, and I probably won't give you one either, and that's probably just as unfair of me as it is of you. I wish we could bury the hatchet, preferrably in your back. Haha, no I take it back, I just want to stop this childish bickering and get back to playing baseball and pitching and winning. I'm starting to feel too old to be fighting teenagers. I wonder what it would be like if I had one of my own.

Do you have any kids, I wonder? and do you treat them like you treat us, especially when we're on the road and we have to sleep down the hallway from your single room while the rest of us get doubles. If you were running the entire show, I'm sure you'd give us quadruples to save hotel money and screw us over and show us who's boss. I'm not a team psychiatrist, I mean I think we have one somewhere around here, but I think just your being around us makes us a worse team because of how we react to you. You never have anything good to say about any of your players, you think obedience and discipline are enough well they're not and it's not helping us become better players. We all think of ways to get rid of you and bump you off though I don't think we really want to kill you we just want you to either leave us alone or change. Maybe you expect too much from us, or maybe you expect too much from yourself and you need everything to be perfect to think you did a good enough job. I can understand that because I always want things to be perfect when I know they can't but you're responsible for the whole team and I just have to worry about me and that's already a lot of worrying.

So what would I say to you if I wasn't drunk like I am now and I could say everything I wanted to say when I needed to say it? Here's what I would say, I would say:

I expect you to use me in situations where you believe I will succeed, and I expect to succeed in situations where you use me. That is all. I don't have to like you because you're my manager, and you don't have to like me because I'm one of your players. We both work for the same boss, but we have different responsibilities. Your job is to organize this team of young talent and develop these players and win ball games by using us in ways in which we can best use our skills. And my job is to do the best I can, whenever and wherever I am.

You got this job for a reason. Somebody upstairs obviously believed you were a good candidate for this managerial position, somebody thought, hey, we need somebody for our new class A team to help those young players of ours and Bill's the guy to do it. I may not be as young as these other guys but I am still a member of this team and it is your duty to treat me the same as you would treat any other member of this team. You don't have to give me the same opportunities as the others — god knows, I've had my share, and I've blown my share. But goddammit, I do not need my own manager constantly backstabbing my every move. It's hard enough trying to second-guess the opposing batter without having to second-guess you.

I'm not trying to tell you how to do your job. I don't want to do your job not right now although maybe later if I ever get a chance. You know how to do your job or else you wouldn't be here. All I want is a fair chance like anybody else, and if I screw up then you have every right not to trust me out on the mound. Look at my numbers so far. Even with a really sore arm, I'm a pretty good pitcher. I'm not the best there ever was, and I'm not the best on the team, but I'm not a bad pitcher, either. I think I proved that today didn't I? If I can't make it on my arm then I have to make it with smarts. I'm not the smartest or the dumbest guy around, I'm probably about as average as you can get well maybe a shade above average but not by much. Maybe I'll never be a big star, well so will a bunch of other people. Even just according to statistics the number of people who make it to the majors is really small, maybe something like 1 in half a million, and there aren't too many stars around these days, I guess there never were too many to begin with or else you couldn't call them stars. But what are the chances of being a star? Probably not too good, maybe 1 in ten million, I don't know. I never really wanted to be a star. Well maybe. It doesn't matter now and you're not helping things, Bill, by being a total prick about everything.

I don't really think I'd say all this stuff to you ever but I just had to write it down. Sometimes when all this stuff stays inside me and starts building up I just have to write it down even though I don't think I write that well. I'm drunk now, so it's even worse, can you tell? Ha. I want so much to do everything better than I can. I want to do well, I don't want to fail, don't you see that? How do you know if you can ever be anybody if you don't know when you fail and when you don't? Who can tell me?

Well that's all I should probably write. My handwriting isn't getting any better either and my eyes hurt almost as bad as my arm now. I hope I remember some of this in the morning. I don't know if I'll be able to read my own handwriting. Maybe I'll think of something better to say.

15

No one on the team heard from Collins during the next few days after the Battle of Batavia, as Lawrence had jokingly called it in the bar that night with the Clippers' starting infielders and left fielder. In fact, Collins had almost mysteriously disappeared, and the team relied on the pitching coach, Kriek, and the batting instructor Rick Tooney for leadership. The two worked in tandem for the game against the Clippers the following night, with Tooney calling the shots on offense from the first base coaching box and Kriek making pitching changes from the dugout, as Hansen and Aguirre combined for a six-hit shutout.

Before the game, the local town newspaper had been gleefully a-buzz about the incident, futilely attempting to interview all the participants, all of whom Kriek and Tooney had strictly forbidden to comment on what had happened. When subsequent penalties became common knowledge soon after the night game, the newspaper came calling again, and again the Wildcats coaches turned the reporters back. Four players were suspended a few games apiece; a few reporters speculated that that was the reason behind the disappearance of the Wildcats' manager from the dugout, but popular rumor in the Wildcat locker room contended that the fiery gentleman had to make a short trip to headquarters in New York City for disciplinary reasons.

On the bus ride late Friday night back to Gladden Fords for a three-game homestand over the weekend, Holforth, who still held a deep grudge, expressed his hope that Collins would lose the job to one of the coaches. Gladly suffering his three-game suspension, Ditch didn't think that would happen, but he did hold out hope for some sort of reprimand. At the very least, the near-riot had given Collins a severe blow to the ego.

Ditch's second newspaper column appeared in the *GF News* Sunday edition, hitting the supermarkets and gas-convenience stores the morning of the last afternoon game of the short series. Mike Grant called Ditch a couple hours before the game to congratulate him on the column's timeliness and writing style: it succinctly described the events on the field leading up to extended scuffle, using a variety of carefully chosen, asterisked-out expletives for humorous effect. He'd decided to leave out the pitch-calling from Collins and did not reproduce any specific dialogue on the field, but he hadn't exactly lied, either, when claiming the fight he had with the Clippers' left fielder began with the offer of an after-game drink. Grant told him over the phone that he received numerous accounts of the incident, none of which he could verify. Ditch didn't offer to clear anything up, and Grant cheerfully took the hint.

As far as Ditch's physical status was concerned, his pitching arm throbbed with pain off and on for two days after his long outing. Spending the pre-game warm-ups on Saturday and Sunday with chemical "ice" packs in hand towels wrapped around his upper arm, He sat in the dugout next to whomever would start the following day, helping him with pitching charts and offering tips on game situations. The younger pitchers actually listened to him, which was a surprise. *Maybe I should have talked to them earlier*, he ruminated.

His arm felt much better Monday night, and Kriek decided he ought to pitch some. After making sure to stretch out between innings, Ditch went in to start the visitors' half of the 7th inning to a cheer of approval from the tiny crowd of perhaps five or six hundred. He pitched slowly to two batters, getting both them to bounce out to the second baseman, and then Kriek removed him for a lefty-lefty confrontation. He received a near-standing ovation as he exited, and, looking up just before stepping down into the dugout, he caught a glimpse of his father, on his feet up in the bleachers behind first base, clapping with a beaming smile.

They left the next day around noon for Fishkill to play the Renegades, the second-year Rangers affiliate, for a July 4th evening contest, and when they reached the Dutchess County Stadium a little after three, they found Collins waiting for them in the parking lot. One by one the players shuffled off the bus with their duffel bags, walking towards the lockers and turning their heads to look at the motionless brown sports-jacketed figure. The manager would not meet anyone's gaze, instead staring blankly at the stadium turnstile entrance, hands in his pants pockets. Near the back of the players' train, Ditch looked over his shoulder and saw the coaches form a semi-circle around Collins, each one with his hands firmly entrenched in his Wildcats' jacket pockets, some slightly pacing and looking at the ground, some already chewing tobacco and spitting. The players continued towards the locker room, and the coaches slowly began to follow. The bus engine whined and shot out a cloud of black exhaust as the driver parked it in the back lot.

Halfway through applying muscle relaxant cream to his pitching arm, Ditch heard Collins call for him. Preparing himself, Ditch tried to nonchalantly make his way towards the visitor's coaches' office; the few players who were still in the locker room studiously ignored him. Collins remained seated behind the barren metal desk, his hat poised precariously on one its rounded corners, as Ditch entered the small room. Three chairs, a metal desk, and Collins, nothing else.

"Close the door and have a seat," Collins said, pushing aside a pile of stat books and charts.

Ditch did so.

The manager folded his hands in front of him. He cleared his throat, but did not look up at Ditch, who sat waiting.

"Our pitching is..." Collins began slowly. He cleared his throat again. "Our starting rotation is in a bind, because of White's injury. It's not serious, the injury I mean, but he'll be out probably at least a week or two still. I've been...I've been told he should stay out for at least two more weeks, to make sure it's completely healed."

He finally looked up. "Until then, however, we're missing a spot from the rotation. Right now we've got Hansen, Lawrence, Porter and Rodriguez. Aguirre started yesterday, as you know, to give Porter an extra day for that slight knee problem of his, and he barely made it through four before we had to take him out."

We, Ditch thought, *in a figurative sense, of course, since you were busy getting chewed out in the City.* He kept his face calm.

Collins opened his mouth to say something else, but closed it and searched in the pile of papers instead. "What I have here..." he said, "what I have here..." He pulled out a spiral bound, brown covered book and flipped through the green quadrille pages. He cleared his throat again and swallowed, as if he was having difficulty speaking. "What I have here are your stats for the season so far.

"Not that I necessarily want you to dwell upon these numbers," he said quickly, "but these numbers are of particular interest."

He ran a finger down a column of figures. "You've got eighteen appearances, all in relief, two of which went past four innings."

He shifted uncomfortably and continued, "In 42 and a third innings, you've let in almost fifty percent of inherited runners. In addition, when you've entered an inning already in progress, your earned run average is well over 5.00, but when you start an inning, it's at 2.80. This says to me..." He closed the book, and swallowed again uncomfortably before concluding, "This says to me that you clearly ought to be a starter."

Ditch felt a flushed thrill of combined anticipation and anxiety, which he immediately suppressed. He hadn't expected this, and he wasn't sure he could fully trust his manager any more. Settling back, he waited for Collins to say something specific.

His manager folded his hands again and stared into space for a moment. Collins' hands began to fidget, and they dived into a pants pocket to bring a handkerchief up to nose-level. Collins quietly blew his nose, wrapped a fist around the cloth and placed the other hand over the fist, before regarding the silent pitcher again.

"Ditch," he said, "I want you to be the fifth starter in the rotation."

Ditch said nothing.

Collins wiped his nose again unnecessarily and made a fist around the handkerchief again. "Now, I know you're not ready to go in today, because you pitched yesterday a bit. So, Porter's going in today, and I'd...I'd like you to start tomorrow when we go back to Gladden Fords and play Elmira."

He closed his mouth firmly and waited for the pitcher to respond. Ditch finally stirred and said, "Okay. It's just that...it's..." He sighed. "Tomorrow's my birthday. It's just...a strange coincidence is all."

Collins almost half-smiled, and the result, in Ditch's view, came very close to a patronizing smirk. "Well," Collins said, "Happy birthday, then."

Ditch had half a mind to say what he had planned to say; the words he had practically rehearsed in his thoughts threatened to push their way out of his vocal cords and into the charged air. It was the air of confrontation, he realized. *I like to fight.*

"Thank you," he said, as sincerely and neutrally as possibly. Collins nodded and motioned that he could go. Ditch did so.

The Wildcats were taking their turn batting when Ditch walked out onto the field. A few eyes turned his way as he made for the bullpen. He could feel the anxiousness in some of the younger players. Porter, the game's starter, was throwing in the pen. He only nodded at Ditch, who returned the nod. Ditch didn't really know the other pitcher, but by all accounts he seemed a quiet, steady guy who kept to himself. Hansen pulled up a chair as Ditch found a seat against the outfield wall.

"So," the tall lefty asked, leaning forward conspiratorially with his elbows on his knees and hands clasped together, "what happened?" The others moved a bit closer but kept their heads down; some stretched their arms over their heads and took glances back at the dugout as if to keep watch.

Ditch leaned back and pulled the bill of his cap up a bit from his eyebrows, choosing his words carefully.

"Well, he showed me some stats and talked about Shawon's hamstring..."

Hansen waited, and then prodded, "Yeah, and then...?"

The sound of Porter's pitches turned Ditch's attention briefly to the catcher in the bullpen a few paces away. Holding the ball an extra moment, Holforth flashed a wicked grin at Ditch from behind the catcher's mask. The subject of Batavia had not come up in recent conversations in hotel rooms, bars or buses; Ditch wondered if there had been simultaneous decisions not to discuss the matter further, or whether a slightly more experienced player had instructed the others to stay quiet about it. *A slightly more experienced player who had an insider's knowledge,* he thought.

He looked back to Hansen, who still awaited a reply.

"Well," he said slowly, taking his cap off and holding it before him like a prayer, "it looks as if I'm gonna be the fifth wheel around here."

Hansen was quietly incredulous for a split second, then let out a restrained whoop and whacked Ditch on the back, shouting, "Yeah, baby, yeah!"

A couple of the relief pitchers congratulated Ditch, unsuccessfully hiding their envy, but all were smiles.

Lawrence shook his hand and clapped him on the back as well. For his part, Ditch couldn't help grinning with delight. The feeling of anxiety had come back, but accompanying it was an older feeling of sheer adolescent excitement, a forgotten emotion of desire.

He got to his feet shakily, almost giddily. Hansen called him an old man and gave him a playful shove; he laughed and shoved back, beginning a jaunt towards the dugout where he would chart the game's pitches. He passed the catcher, still in the receiving end of the bullpen, pointed an accusing finger and declared his intent to have a short investigative discussion after the game. Holforth made no reply other than a brief laugh, and Ditch continued towards the dugout.

At the top of the steps, on the opposite side from the bat rack, White was sitting on the ground, leaning against the outside post of the dugout with his legs resting easily spread out in front of him. His right leg bore a soft cast from hip to ankle, metal outside supports with velcro straps. Ditch slowed his pace upon seeing the injured pitcher, not knowing if he should talk to him. He couldn't describe the normally outgoing pitcher as "withdrawn" and the slight change in White's demeanor hadn't yet elicited any "you're not like yourself" comments from his teammates, but there was a sense of anger in him that made Ditch hesitate to approach. *A sense of self-anger*, he thought.

"Hey, wussup, big guy," Ditch tried, stepping down to the dugout bench. White didn't turn his head, kept staring out at the batting cage.

"I dunno, man," he replied. "My butt hurts, been sitting here a half hour already."

Ditch didn't reply at first, searching for the pitching charts. He found them in a folder-clipboard under a warm-up jacket on the bench. "Uh...you want me to get you a chair or something?" he said. "Get you off the ground, you want."

White started shaking his head, then stopped and briefly reached up to adjust the bill of his cap. "Yeah, sure," he mumbled. "Thanks, man."

"Not a problem." Ditch wandered back to the bullpen and returned with a chair. Pushing himself to his feet unaided, White allowed Ditch to place the chair behind him and then sat down with hands in pockets, the same expression on his face of barely disguised frustration.

Ditch stood there for a few minutes, taking out a fresh sheet of paper and preparing it for the game, noting the teams and players, the dimensions of the field. If he knew the wind speed and direction and the temperature, he'd mark them down, too. Every little bit helped, and he could never be sure which bit it would be. Next to him White maintained silent vigil over his field of vision.

After a moment Ditch spoke again. "How's the leg?"

White didn't respond right away. Finally he replied, "Dunno. Feels twingy in the morning, hurts going down stairs." He paused and added as a statement, "Heard you got the spot."

"Yeah." Ditch closed the folder and squatted down. "Yeah," he repeated, "Bill called me in just now and told me. Must've got his balls handed to him in New York, 'cause he didn't look none too happy about it."

White looked at him sideways and then back to the field. "Yeah, tell me 'bout it."

"Yeah, well..." Ditch stopped himself as he was about to make another comment on White's injury, to the effect that he would be over it soon enough and have his starting role back. *It's like he's never been injured like this before*, he thought. *Maybe he's just not dealing with it.*

He coughed and changed his train of thought. "Yeah, well, they got me doing the charts today."

"Yeah? We ain't playing these guys tomorrow."

"Yeah, but we are the day after. You know, we're here one day, then home against one team for a day, then home against these guys again, and then we get a day off before three more games against the guys tomorrow."

He paused. "It's like, even though everything's scheduled, when it happens, it all comes as a surprise anyways, doesn't it?"

He held up his twice-broken finger, awkwardly curled up under the pencil in his right hand. White glanced at him and slowly nodded, lowering his head. Ditch patted him on the shoulder, got to his feet and began to head over to get a better look at the batters as the opposing team took their turn in the cage.

"Hey, Ditch," White called, "can I get a piece of that paper from you?"

Ditch returned and obliged. "What for?"

"I'm gonna keep my own book, you know," White said, "so I'm gonna need my own clipboard and pencil and folder and shit. You know what I'm saying?"

"Yeah, I do." Ditch reached out with a hand to drag White to his feet. "C'mon over to the cage with me."

"What for?"

Ditch nodded towards the cage. The Renegades' hitters had started slapping softly lobbed pitches through the clay infield. White tried to refuse help, but had to place an arm around Ditch's shoulders for support as the two walked and Ditch patiently began to explain the goals for the pitcher's strategic espionage.

16

Some time after one in the morning, John stood on the edge of the outfield grass, still wearing his baseball uniform pants, holding a mostly empty fifth of whiskey in one hand and an old cloth bag of practice balls in the other, wondering hazily what on earth he was doing there.

The game had not gone quite as planned; he had made it through five innings, but the birthday announcement over the public speakers and crowd singing Happy Birthday at the top of their lungs while he was preparing to throw to the first batter of the game shattered his concentration at the outset. Four runs scored, two unearned, before he regained control in the third. He allowed no more, and luckily the opposing pitcher let in two in each of the first four, so he left a winner. But he didn't feel it. Legions of fans, especially children, lining up at the fence just prior to the after-game fireworks hadn't made him feel any better. Hansen, Lawrence, and Corrales were the most popular targets for autograph-seekers, but they dragged John out of the clubhouse to give his John Hancock, too. He signed caps, game programs, pennants, the back of somebody's shirt, even a half-empty popcorn container.

His father had stayed to the end, waiting at the back of the crowd. After the signing session was over, he slowly made his way down the bleachers, leaning over the fence near the dugout during the fireworks display. John leaned back against the fence from the other side, arms crossed. The fireworks shot up from the small workers' lot at the back of the stadium, smoke drifting outward in the rapidly cooling July night air over the playing field and stands as his father spoke about the evening's performance. He could have done better, his father said helpfully, he could have done this or that and thought about this and that. He did well, he won as a starter, but he might want to keep some things in mind for next time, and he might improve.

John thought his father said all that. He must have, John thought, staring across the field, his eyes still getting used to the darkness of a stadium with no lights. Hadn't he always criticized before? Hadn't he always had something negative to say, how John just wasn't good enough, and wasn't there always room for improvement? He thought so, John thought so.

He closed his eyes and took a swig from the whiskey. He'd found the bottle in his locker, after saying goodbye to his parents and family in attendance at the park. They mentioned something about a birthday party over the weekend, and he remembered shrugging with a smile and thinking about outdoor picnics with relatives he'd never heard of before and little cousins running around like rabbits. The bottle had a note attached to it, from Mike, saying he'd give a call on Thursday night or Friday and see if he wanted to have a little get together with old high school friends, more people John didn't know, or didn't remember. He had wondered how Mike had smuggled the thing into the park, and then had opened the fifth and begun to dissolve into eighty proof. Ooohhhh, Cap'n Jack'll getchu high t'night...he crooned to the darkness.

The bag dropped to the ground, a few balls popped out and rolled a short distance away on the dewy grass as John finished one long swallow and then emptied the bottle. He let it sway in his grip at knee-height before plunking to his feet. The smoke from the fireworks still seemed to linger, hiding in wisps of gray in the outfield corners and along the foul line walls and dugouts. A breeze, slightly stronger than it had been at game time, quietly swirled from between third and home out to right-center. The infield dirt, watered down before and after the game to prevent miniature dust storms in the week-long dry spell, gave off ankle-high spurts of sand, tendrils licking the backs of John's legs where he stood between first and second on the edge of the outfield grass.

The figure of a man towered before him. A tall man, high in the saddle, who wore a tall hat and held his lasso high above his head, solidly struck in a pose of utter confidence. John squinted at the figure before him, standing above the right field wall advertisements of First National Bank and Stewart's Ice Cream. A face etched with deep lines of strength and unyielding power. He hated it. He hated it with all his being, he hated it down from the sky to the earth below that he might crush it beneath his feet and grind it to nothingness.

John stooped and plucked a brown baseball from the open bag. Unsteadily straightening again, he clutched the ball in his right hand, feeling for the worn red threads stitching the old leather together. He relaxed his grip, not taking his eyes from the figure of contempt in the approaching distance, sliding the threads to his fingertips.

This, he said, is the curveball I should have thrown to Conroy in the top of the first. And he wound his arm over his head, and, stepping forward onto the slick outfield grass, flung the ball with all his might towards the figure. His arm flailed in front of him as he staggered off balance and caught himself, hearing a faint wooden thud as the ball caromed off the outfield wall.

He straightened and swayed. The figure loomed

larger. He reached for another ball and held it before him, aiming to put another cleft in the unprotected chin. And this, he shouted, is the fastball I should have thrown high and inside to McCloskey. The ball soared through the air and disappeared over the wall to the figure's left, falling into the murkiness of the woods beyond. When will it end? John wondered, repeating it out loud. When will it end? The figure grew closer, demanding, when are you going to get married, son? When are you going to give us our first grandchildren? All your brothers look up to you, you know, they all look up to you.

No, stop, he said in a low voice. The figure persisted, mocking, goading, spoiling for a fight. Why don't you listen, why don't you call? You know, you can see the father through the son, whenever you look at the son you see the father in him. I'm sorry, John said back, grasping another ball with a desperate fist, I'm sorry I can't... Just be yourself, the words floated to him, pounding at him, forcing their way into his skull, pounding. Make me proud, your mother and brothers listen to every game on the radio, send us the newspaper articles, we tell all our neighbors about you, we're always watching you, you're our son, our oldest son, our oldest...

No! John cried. The slider to Rogers in the third, men on first and third with two outs, arced through the fog and struck the pack of cigarettes, a metallic clang as it rebounded back to the field and bounced to a halt near the foul line. He reached for another ball and a final whisper reached John's ears, All we want is for you to be happy...

He let the ball drop back into the bag. A swampy sensation had invaded his head above his eye sockets and at the back of his head near the neck. Groggily he glanced about for random balls, found a couple, and was satisfied enough to forget those he knew had been left behind somewhere. He accidentally kicked the bottle as it lay on the damp grass. He hefted it, poised to project it over the outfield wall, and against all better judgment decided against it. Slowly, steadily, John carried the ball bag back towards the clubhouse where he got it, dropping the bottle into a garbage can in the dugout.

I'm drunk, he thought distantly, but I never get that drunk. He supposed he should feel some pride at his self-restraint, but all he felt was tired. He turned at the edge of the dugout, looking back across the field at the shadowy figure, still standing, wavering in the breeze, above the wall, impervious to assault, unflinching in its resolve. Some day, he thought, some day, it would come down. And he would still be here. And he turned and walked down into the clubhouse, and then home.

17

On the day following Ditch's first start, Paul Hansen threw a five-hit shutout. The following Wednesday, Hansen was gone, called up to Class AA Binghamton.

"The call" itself came Sunday after the second game at Vermont. The way Hansen explained it to Ditch in his hotel room that night, he'd been told that after the All-Star Break in the majors, a couple of guys from Class AAA were getting the call, which meant a few players from each level were being bumped up a notch. Ditch knew the call-up would further weaken their staff, and he would miss Hansen and his annoyingly loud punk music, but these things inevitably happened. It was just another reminder that winning and losing were secondary to development of prospects in the minors.

That last night with Hansen in the Best Western, one of the guys, Ditch couldn't remember which one, suggested they do something "special" for Hansen's last road game — or, at least, his last road game before the long bus ride back to Gladden Fords. There were five of them there in Ditch's hotel room — Reynalds, Lawrence,

Hansen, Holforth, and Ditch, lying back comfortably on a bed since, of course, it was his room. His roommate Aguirre was missing, maybe down in the lobby playing cards, or maybe just down the hallway in someone else's room, he didn't know. Or maybe he was getting ready for "the call," himself. The Wildcats had already lost three position players in addition to Hansen. But that's what the minors were for, after all. No player knew how long he would have the same teammates, all competing for the same chances.

White was still keeping to himself, reading a book in his room, and they all decided not to bother him, saying that if he wanted to sulk, he could go ahead and sulk. For the few who had bonded, however briefly, it was time to celebrate a teammate's good fortune.

Question was, what could they do in the bustling metropolis of downtown Burlington, Vermont? It was too late in the afternoon to play golf, even if Reynalds and Holforth could have convinced the others to join them. "No way are you getting me out on some rich man's playground," Lawrence said. "Look, I hit the ball, and then I walk after it, and then I hit it again, and then I walk after it some more. Uh-uh."

"Well," Ditch asked, "how about miniature golf?"

Lawrence just looked at him, and Ditch shrugged.

"Just making a suggestion."

Montreal was a possibility, since it was only about two hours away — definitely at least two hours if they used his car, Holforth said — but they weren't sure they had enough money to afford staying there overnight. Of course, Collins would probably blow his top at them for leaving town at all, and they would probably be lucky to get back into town barely in time for the next night's game, so reluctantly they crossed that off as an option. The same for visiting Ethan Allen's historic campsite, or boat launch, or whatever it was that Ditch couldn't quite remember, having last been there fifteen years previous.

Once again, bar-hopping was an option, but that didn't strike any of them as particularly "special." Besides, Holforth said, that was all they did anyway, to which they could only agree, all knowing full well Hansen's aversion to the bar scene in the first place. Ditch recalled Holforth's suspicion that Hansen's religion prevented him from enjoying alcohol, although to all appearances White's adamant Christianity hadn't prevented him from tipping a few. Ditch supposed everyone had their own interpretations of religion, and as long as no one tried to convert him, that was perfectly fine with him.

His mind had wandered during the ongoing conversation and when he surfaced again for some reason they were all sitting at the edges of the two beds discussing their salaries. Someone had brought up Hansen's signing bonus, Ditch figured. Reynalds was in the process of describing what he termed a "typical player's career," and subsequent arbitrations and other legal money matters.

"...so after the first three years, you go to arbitration, which everyone knows the players win..." Reynalds was saying.

Holforth interrupted, "Who's 'everyone'?"

"Uh, well, you know, the experts, the agents. Why else would the union agree to salary arbitration? Right, so, if you're not a 'star player,' like Paul here, by the time you're, say, 27 or 28, you're making three hundred thousand, right? Now, I figure if I can stick it out here at my present salary..."

Holforth interrupted again, "Whadid you say you was making?"

"Twenty thou."

"Okay, I'm making about $18,000, maybe a bit more. Larry, what about you?"

"I don't know, around sixteen, I think. Hey, anybody mind if I put the TV on?"

Ditch shrugged. "Go ahead. No cable, though, so alls

we get is a couple local channels, PBS I think, from Montreal."

"No way, hotel's got to have cable." Lawrence was at the set on top of the short wooden dressers, fiddling with the wobbling channel dial.

Holforth continued his interrogation. "Ditch?"

Ditch paused, not wanting to admit anything. They had been ordered by the manager and all the coaches not to talk about salaries, on the grounds that money always created team tensions. But that wasn't his reason. "About eighteen, give or take a thousand," he said carefully. After eight years in the professionals, he should be making more, and they all must have realized that.

There was a slight pause in the group conversation. "Okay, now Paul, what are you making?" Holforth asked.

"Uh, well," the teenager shoved his hands in his pockets, "the agent told my father the bonus was a couple hundred thousand or something like that, but I haven't seen any of it. I think I get something like $30,000."

Reynalds smirked as he tapped a cigarette out of a Marlboro Lights soft pack and tucked it behind his ear. He was clearly irritated at Ditch's no-smoking policy in the room. He pulled out a lighter and flicked it once or twice, saying, "Now, see, that's the 'star player' career track. You keep on going, and you'll be making at least five million by the time we're all making maybe two hundred thou."

"That's if any of us get up to the Majors," Ditch said sardonically. They fell silent, Holforth nodding his head. After a flick or two more, Reynalds pocketed the lighter. "...Paul included,' Ditch added. Paul was looking at the television screen, where Lawrence had found the Three Stooges.

A prolonged silence spread throughout the room. The sound of a loud fuzzy radio reception and laughter from the adjacent rooms informed Ditch of the location of his roommate. Aguirre and Corrales and a couple others probably were playing cards and smoking and listening to the Spanish station from Montreal. He spoke after a moment, "Say, Rick, where'd you get all these numbers? This from that pamphlet I saw you reading in the dugout the other day?"

Reynalds nodded. "Yeah. It's called 'The Baseball Industry in 1995.' One of my friends back home saw it in a Harvard Business School report and mailed it to the clubhouse last week."

"So," Lawrence said from his spot near the TV, "all you think about is the 'baseball industry'? Man, it's no wonder things are bad up there."

"No, that's not it," Reynalds started to protest. They'd all heard about the drop in attendance in both the American and National Leagues. Some of Ditch's friends and neighbors had told him they "boycotted" the three-week delayed Opening Day, by not watching it on TV, in retaliation for the strike and the cancellation of the 1994 post-season. Many former fans boycotted the game in actuality, and many continued to stay home from major league games, although it hadn't seemed to affect minor league attendance.

"If it's not the money, then what are you doing here, man?" Lawrence asked. "All I hear from you is how we're all idealists and all that bullshit. What's up with all that? You a complete mercenary or what?"

"Hey, that ain't fair," Holforth said as Reynalds attempted to respond. "We all make money, right? It *is* a job, right?"

"Yeah," Reynalds finally got in, "but, see..." He took a deep breath. "It's my father. He's this big stockbroker, and my mom's a professor at UConn, and the two of them paid my way through Yale, right? I mean, I'm pretty smart..."

"Uh huh, you're a regular Brainiac," Hansen immediately said. Lawrence and Holforth howled. "Okay, wiseass, sure, whatever," Reynalds said somewhat fiercely, but a grin broke out of the snarl and he laughed a bit before sombering up again and continuing, "Look, I got into Yale, right? So my father thinks that since he put me through one of the best colleges in the world, I should be making tons of money right now. I majored in marketing and finance, I oughta be working on Wall Street with him, raking in the dough."

He paused and Ditch picked up the thread, "So, you think you have to show him you can make a lot of money playing baseball. Is that it?"

Reynalds nodded.

"You know, that's pretty dumb. But," Ditch added, seeing Reynalds start to protest again, "I can understand it. You guys, you're all five to ten years younger than me, and you're making about the same. According to your business predictions, I should be in six digits now, right?"

"Okay, but then why are you still playing?" Hansen asked. "I heard you were gonna be a replacement player. Would you still do it?"

On the television screen Curly had just accidentally stuck a radiator tube in his mouth, thinking it the end of a skunk weed pipe. "I don't know," Ditch finally said, looking at his folded hands. "I just...you know, it's not the money. I work during the off-season 'cause I can't get any of the winter league teams interested. I've worked in the post office, and in restaurants, and as a UPS truck driver and a bartender and a waiter and a dishwasher. But baseball...it's not the money, it's baseball."

He looked up. "You know, in the minors, it doesn't matter who wins; we're all here to try to get out of here. Up in the Majors, that's where it all counts. And it's still not the wins that count, not really, because if you lose one day you can come back and win the next day. There's so many games to play."

He paused and the sound of the radio in the room next door seemed to grow louder for a moment. None of the others had moved. Ditch felt he had to continue, although he knew it was turning into somewhat of a sermon. "It's...I remember putting on the Rangers uniform, and walking down that concrete corridor to the playing field for practice. And coming in from the bullpen, watching someone open the outfield padded doors and running across the outfield in front of twenty thousand fans. I was on that mound, and all the guys you see on TV were all there, and they all looked just like the guys you knew in high school. It was..."

He sighed. "I'm not getting back up there again. I know that. Some of you guys are, in a couple years, maybe. But I gotta do my best. I just have to, you know? I love baseball, and I'm sure those guys making all the money do, too. It doesn't matter how much you get paid, ten thousand, fifty, two hundred, two million, the game's the same. If you're in it for the money, you're playing a different game."

There was an extended pause and uncomfortable shuffling on the bed by Reynalds and Holforth. Hansen and Lawrence were sitting on the floor at the ends of the beds, watching the Stooges. Ditch got up. "Look, I'm sorry guys, I didn't mean to go off like that. I'm no expert or anything."

"Hey, man, that's all right," Lawrence said.

"Yeah," said Holforth. "So...what're we gonna do tonight? Watch the fucking TV all night long?"

Hansen thought for a second and then turned to Ditch. "Why don't we, like, play a prank or something? You know, like the other day in Watertown?"

Ditch laughed and shook his head, recalling the scene in the hotel when Holforth came up late after spending almost ten dollars in quarters on "Virtua Fighter II" in the lobby. He had been opening the door to his room when he had discovered a slimy white-translucent film on the doorknob. He had let out a groan and turned towards the bathroom when Ditch had emerged with a toothbrush in his mouth, asking if Holforth had seen the last issue of *Hustler*.

"That wudn't no prank," Holforth said, "that was just disgusting."

"Yeah, but it was funny."

"Well, I read something somewhere," Ditch began. He paused to think about it, and then shook his head. "Nah. Forget it. Probably wouldn't work."

Hansen grabbed his arm. "Oh, no, you gotta tell us now."

Holforth and Lawrence stood, crowding around him in anticipation. Ditch rubbed his chin thoughtfully. "Well, I don't know if it's going to work, but...okay, anybody got any rope?"

"Rope?" asked Reynalds, still sitting on one of the beds. "What kinda stupid question is that?"

"Okay, okay, never mind. Maybe we can use sheets." Ditch walked over to the unoccupied bed and stripped it. "All right, each bed has two sheets. Everyone go grab the sheets off their beds and bring 'em into the bathroom. And check the closets, too, bring all the sheets you can find."

"Whatever you say, man," said Lawrence. Reynalds slowly rolled off the bed, and Ditch proceeded to strip that one as well. Rolling the sheets under his arm, he slipped out into the hallway and headed for the bathroom at the end of the hallway. *This would probably work better if each room in this cheap hotel had their own bathroom,* he thought. He just hoped the five could manage to be quiet enough not to attract the attention of everyone else in the hallway. He paused for a second outside Corrales' door. The radio was louder than ever, and the laughter and bursts of rapid Spanish were increasingly loud. Somebody had a bottle of something, he figured, reaching the bathroom and flicking the light on.

The others came all at once, dragging their sheets behind them. White was there by now, Lawrence explaining that he couldn't very well leave his roommate out of it, since he needed the sheets. Holforth and Hansen were roommates, and Reynalds' roommate was in the room with Alfonse and Aguirre and two other Caribbean players. The rest of the team appeared to be either already sleeping or watching the local news on TV in their respective rooms, though Ditch knew some of them, three or four, probably, must have gone out to at least try to find something to do on a late Sunday afternoon in a small town.

Trying to keep his posse quiet, Ditch motioned that they should tie the sheet corners together. He turned the sink faucet on and ran the sheets under the water an inch at a time. Occasionally a knot would untie and he would have to tie it back together, whispering, "You call that a knot?" Hansen jumped in and helped him with the tangle of wet sheets accumulating on the floor to his left, but the others simply stood in the doorway, trying to see what Ditch was doing.

"Get back!" he rasped. "Collins might see us all."

"What're you doing?" Holforth said.

Ditch hissed. "Keep it down!" He peered over Reynalds' head down the hallway. Water was slopping over the bathroom floor and would likely run out onto the worn blue carpet. Too late, he realized he should have done this in the tub. The task of wringing out the sheets was taking too long; fifteen minutes into it and there were still a couple sheets completely soaking wet.

Handing one end to Lawrence, Ditch motioned to tie it to the nearest doorknob. Lawrence whispered to him, "I think I got what you're doing." Reynalds and Holforth dragged the soggy mass behind, trying to loop the sheets around the doorknobs as quietly as possible. Again, Ditch made more motions: pull the knots as tight as possible, crossing from one door to its opposite across the hallway, then diagonally across to another. They made sure to open Ditch's door slightly so they could slip back into it, and deliberately left the manager's door alone.

Ditch wasn't sure if Collins was in the room, but he didn't want to take the chance. He'd already been in plenty of hot water with the man, and things were just beginning to look up. The rest of the team, however, was fair game.

They finished, running out of sheets after nine doors. There was a bit left over after the last door, so Hansen wrapped whatever was left around the knob as many times as possible in a gigantic knot. They quietly crawled on the floor underneath the criss-crossing, dripping wet sheets back to Ditch's door. "Now what?" Hansen asked.

"Okay," Ditch instructed, pointing next door. "Now, you bang on the door and tell them there's a call downstairs in the lobby."

"Me?"

"Sure. This is your party." Ditch gave him a grin, and they all ducked into the room while Hansen rapped next door and spoke in a loud voice, "Hey! Phone call for Corrales!" He had to repeat it three times before someone in the room turned the radio down and heard. Quickly, Hansen fled into Ditch's room, and they carefully pushed the door shut. It would ease the slack a little bit, but the sheets would still be tight enough to prevent anyone from opening the door more than a crack.

Which is exactly what happened, if the sounds next

door were any indication. Holforth tried to translate the loud cursing which accompanied the pounding on the door. "Okay, here we go...what the fuck...motherfucking son-of-a-whore...um...something about your cousin...and a dog...no, a donkey..."

The rest of the hallway heard the shouting, and, upon trying their own doors, commenced their own shouting. After a couple of minutes, the manager's voice could be heard booming down the hallway, "What in Christ's name is going on here?"

They couldn't help it. The six of them began laughing hysterically. Hansen doubled up and fell on the floor, holding his arms crossed underneath him as his face got red from laughter. Lawrence was holding his chest and tears were streaking down his face, as was the case with Reynalds. Holforth had begun to repeat in extremely bad Spanish the curses from next door, and followed each one with increasingly high-pitched laughter. White himself was trying very hard not to aggravate his injured leg as he staggered about the room howling.

Ditch thought he heard Collins going door to door trying to unpry the sheets from the doorknobs and swearing profusely when he couldn't budge them an inch. But Ditch was too busy looking out the window at Corrales, who had opened his own window and was hurriedly climbing down the back fire escape to the street below.

"Ssshhit," Holforth gasped between fits of laughter, "I hope the guy don't kill himself."

"Jesus, Ditch," Reynalds laughed, "this is the best fucking stunt I've ever seen."

"Read it in a book, like I said," Ditch replied as they quieted down to an occasional outburst. "See, all the doors open inward, right? And the water only makes knots tighter when you pull on them."

"Pure genius, man!" cried Hansen "Oh, man, I can't stop laughing. It hurts."

There was a pounding at the door. "Open up in there!" Collins demanded. "What in God's name is going on here? Open this goddamn door!"

"Sorry, Coach!" called White. "Can't! It's stuck!" They all burst into laughter again as Collins swore and pounded the door.

Ditch got up and tried to pull the door open. It moved about two inches and held swaying as Collins glared in through the crack. "Who was responsible for this?" he demanded.

"Well, Mr. Collins," Ditch smiled, "way I hear it, it's all Tom Seaver's fault." The five behind him burst into another brief fit of hysteria. Collins stared at him. "I'm not kidding, Coach. I read it in his book."

Collins took a deep breath and let it out. He leaned against the door, and it didn't even budge as the sheets behind him let out a high-pitched whining sound like a mouse squeak. "You mean this wasn't your idea?" he asked in a lower voice.

"Nope. Sorry," Ditch shrugged. "Guess I'm not just all that original."

Collins tried to look into the room and pulled his head back out again. "You know," he said, lowering his voice even more, "I'm surprised you got this trick to work. I tried it once in Wisconsin and all the damn sheets fell apart." He smiled and backed away, saying in a normal tone of voice, "All right, you had your fun, boys. Now get out here and untie this mess so the hotel doesn't throw us all out on the street."

Ditch grinned and began closing the door. "Here. I'll cut you some slack." Reynalds and Lawrence started chuckling again, and it caused the others to laugh, which caused the originators to laugh even harder. Ditch closed the door, and listening through it, he could hear the muffled sound of Collins laughing quietly to himself as he slowly, and a great deal of effort, untied the first water-drenched knot.

18

John's alarm went off at 10 am Friday morning, July the 21st, only the second off-day of the season. He got out of bed at nearly 11:30, having reflexively hit the snooze bar a number of times. Yawning and stretching, John slowly shuffled out to the living room and pulled back the shutters which covered the sliding glass doors. He'd left them turned open in front of the screen window, where he'd placed a large square metal fan on top of a footstool to try to get some air circulation in the apartment. The balcony from the apartment above sheltered his own balcony a bit from the sun, but it felt like 90 degrees already, another scorcher of a day.

Luckily for him, he'd pitched the previous day at night, the seven o'clock start allowing for a game time temperature of 85, a full ten degrees cooler than the temperature at noon. Playing baseball at night was something he never quite had gotten used to, being somewhat of a baseball purist, but he had to admit that the cooler temps as the game wore on had come as a relief.

Now, with the sun still reaching its apex, the stage was about to be set for an afternoon outdoor barbeque. The Wildcats manager had thankfully called off practice, saying that they all needed a restful, relaxing day, so John had invited some friends over for good old American hamburgers and hotdogs. He suggested they come over around one or one-thirty; one of the disadvantages of playing minor league ball was that they could never really watch any afternoon games on television, since they were usually playing the afternoon games of their own, but John supposed they could find some game on somewhere. A Cubs game, if nothing else. You could always rely on an afternoon game at Wrigley, he knew.

After a short shower John headed over to the local IGA and bought fresh meat and the appropriate condiments. Holding the case of Michelob on his shoulder with one hand and carrying in a white plastic bag the ground chuck, chips, rolls and two-liter cherry cola with the other, he walked on cracked light gray sidewalks with weeds growing between the uneven slabs of pock-marked concrete, lined with meridians of dry dirt where grass once grew. Overhead the light blue sky beat down in waves, July haze rippling along the faded streets. Wispy cirrus clouds lay strung out in long arcing bundles of threads, a sign of the weekend storm to come, hopefully after the team had already left by bus for

Williamsport, Pennsylvania.

John reveled in the heat. It wasn't just hot weather, it was the laziness of the hot weather, the salty sweat it caused by your simply being outside, the involuntary relaxing of tense muscles, the natural outdoor sauna. The warm breeze that swirled upwards from the parking lot behind the apartment building, the sound of neighborhood children running up and down the streets. The hum of radios in adjacent apartments and receding boom of car stereos, the smell of mown grass in small square backyards and cooked red meat on charcoal briquettes on backdoor patios. This was summer, and he loved every minute of it.

Just before one he put the TV on and watched the end of the noon newshour on channel 6, WRGB, out of Albany. Yes, the weathercaster confirmed there was a storm system headed their way, but it wouldn't hit until Saturday night into Sunday afternoon. It might threaten the game in Auburn on Sunday, he thought. Strange road trips they had, one game away at one place, then another the very next day in a town four hours away. The jerking, lurching bus rides seemed endless. The best thing about the end of July in New York, he decided, was that it was usually storm-free, and when there were storms, they moved through violently and quickly.

He picked up the can of lighter fluid which rested

just outside the screen door and squirted a liquid covering over the pyramid of briquettes in the red-lid covered barbeque grill. Checking his watch, John figured he'd have about half an hour before anyone showed up. Twenty or twenty-five minutes before the grill was ready, maybe ten minutes at most for the food. He went back inside to the kitchen, opened the fridge and cracked open a beer. Not quite cold yet, but cold enough he decided, walking back towards the open balcony door and giving the briquettes a second liberal dousing before touching matches to two or three spots.

Half an hour later, after the charcoal had settled in a smoldering bed of gray ash, Eric and Rick arrived. Out on the balcony forming the hamburger into flattened round patties, John walked over to the door with a ball of meat in his hands, calling for the two to open the door. Hey, guys, breakfast will be ready in a few minutes here, he said, motioning towards the kitchen with an elbow. There's beer, in the fridge. Go ahead and grab a couple if you want to.

That reporter here yet? Eric asked as he popped open a can and sat down heavily on the black plastic couch in front of the TV. Rick was walking behind the couch towards the balcony to give an extra can to John. Thanks, John said, wiping his hands clean on a dishrag which hung tied from a handle on the grill. No, Mike's not here yet. He said he'd be over sometime around 2 or 3, he wasn't sure when he'd get off for lunch. Larry and Shawon coming? He put a few hotdogs on the grill and came back into the living room with the tongs in one hand and his beer in the other. ESPN was on, showing a celebrity golf game in Hawaii. What is this crap? he asked.

Cubs don't start for another half hour, Eric said. They're in the Central Time Zone, remember.

Oh. Yeah. John headed for the kitchen, crossing in front of the couch and momentarily blocking their vision of the screen. I think I got some paper towels or napkins, but I don't know if there's any paper plates.

'Sokay, Rick said, finishing his first can. We're slobs, we don't mind. Get me another beer?

Sure. Eric, want another one?

Yeah, cool. Uh...Larry said he'd be here soon. I think he wanted to stop and get some soda and chips or something.

I already got some, John said, returning to the living room with fresh cans. He kept walking out to the balcony to check the barbecue's progress. What about Shawon?

Well, Rick said, I heard he got up kind of early and went to the ballpark to practice.

Really?

Yeah. He's kind of antsy about coming back. I heard they want him to sit out another week, but he wants to start pitching tomorrow or Sunday. He's doing lots of sprints, must stretch out like a dozen times a day.

Yeah, Eric said, he's got this whole routine now...hey, Rick, I just noticed something. Where's your smokes?

Uh, I quit.

Yeah? For real?

Rick shifted uncomfortably on the couch. Yeah, sort of. I still got a pack in the hotel room, but I only smoked a couple over the past week.

Huh, Eric said.

They were all quiet for a few moments. Eric searched for the remote, and then started flipping through the channels one at a time, never resting on any of them long enough to determine what was showing. John stood out on the balcony, occasionally turning the hotdogs, taking a sip from his beer. The sounds of traffic, the whine of passing engines and quick braking for the stop sign at the nearby intersection was lost amid the sizzle of the grill and the low beat of the rap music video Eric had finally settled on.

There was a short series of bangs on the metal door, and Dave walked in, carrying a brown grocery bag. Hey, this where the party's at? he said, throwing a folded newspaper at Eric. Check out that little article on page C7. Funny as shit. I just stood there laughing in the store. Woman at the register probably thought I was a crazy...

That why you took so long? Eric said, searching through the paper. Hey, it's all outta order.

Yeah, Dave said, I already read most of it waiting in line. Hey, where should I put this stuff? Hey, John?

Yeah, John called from the balcony, leave it on the kitchen table in there. What'd you get? Chips and stuff?

You got it. Garlic and onions, got some tortillas and salsa.

Christ, Rick mumbled. Looks like we're gonna get a nice breeze coming through here. Eric started laughing. Hell, it wasn't that funny, Rick said.

No, Eric said, listen to this article. This is great. There's this team in the Appalachian rookie league, right? And a guy on the team they were playing got hit in from second base, by a double or whatever. Anyways, he missed home plate and the catcher let the ball get away from him and it rolled to the backstop.

This is good. Listen to this, Dave said, opening a bag of chips and offering it to Rick.

Eric continued, Okay, so the pitcher is at home by now, right? and he yells at the catcher that the runner missed the plate. So, instead of throwing him the ball, the catcher...get this...the catcher runs at the guy in the dugout. The guy's taking his helmet off, and he panics and starts running back towards the plate, and then the third baseman on the field runs to the plate and yells at the catcher to throw him the ball. The catcher's like almost in the other team's dugout by now, so he turns around and throws it to the third baseman. The runner turns around and heads back for the dugout. And the third baseman throws the ball back to the catcher.

I don't believe this, Rick said. Gimme that, I gotta read this.

No way, lemme finish, Eric said, holding the paper away from Rick's swipe at it. Here, I'll read what it says. He scanned the article, his mouth moving silently as he read. Okay, here we go...And so, when all that was called for was a tag on home plate, the Lumberjacks third baseman and catcher caught the Hawks outfielder in a run-down between home and the visiting team's dugout...

Dave and Rick began to crack up.

...a run-down which lasted almost five minutes...Eric laughed and had to put the paper down. Oh, God, that is so stupid.

Better frame that one, John said, coming in from the balcony with a stack of hamburgers in rolls. Sorry about the hands, hope you guys don't mind. There's ketchup and mustard if anybody needs it.

Mustard, on burgers? Dave said, offering John the chips. What is this, McDonald's?

That's right, John said, it's John's Baseball Burgerworld. You know what that article reminded me just now...

I know, Eric interrupted, Frank screwing up that one night in Ontario, when he was halfway up the baseline instead of at the plate waiting for the throw.

Yeah, Rick said, I almost died laughing at first base when he let the ball hit him in the head and bounce into the screen. Oh, man, that was a riot.

Well, I hope Mike doesn't get wind of some of this stuff. I don't want him writing about what he calls inside material. He ever got hold of that sheet-tying incident...

Aw, c'mon, Eric complained, some of this'd be great

if somebody wrote it down. You still do that column, right?

Yeah, man, Dave put in, why don't you write about some of this? This stuff would make some good reading.

No, John replied. No, I'm still in enough hot water with Bill, plus my dad makes a habit out of cutting out every single article I write and every boxscore my name appears in. He sticks them all over the fridge at ho...at my parents' house.

Hey, that's right, your parents live right here in town, Rick said. Sometimes I see your father up in the stands, but I've never seen your mother. You stop by to visit them after home games?

Yeah, I stop by once in a while to mow the lawn for him, visit my little sister, John said. But, you know, it just feels too weird to be there for too long. Almost like there's a different family in the house.

Yeah, what's up with that, Eric asked. You got how many kids in your family?

Seven, only two at home now. Well, maybe three if you count Craig. He's here and gone, every time one of his women throw him out on the street.

Jesus, haven't your parents ever heard of, you know, birth control?

Hey, Rick, I'm not going to tell my parents what to do. Shit, it feels weird just talking about it. My mom just says it's because they're Irish Catholic.

Hang on, Dave said. Your last name, isn't it Jewish or something?

Well, it can be. Jonathan Klein isn't exactly a rare name. It's German, but it's not my father's real last name. He was adopted when he was a kid, after his real father died in an accident or something. John took another bite of his hotdog. Anybody want more? Still half a package left. And there's still tons of beer left, too. He got up from the couch and wandered back outside to the grill.

And, uh...he continued, that's kinda where my, uh, nickname comes from.

Yeah? Dave called from inside. I heard a couple stories about it.

Really? Where?

Well, you know, just around. I heard that it's because you used to work as a grave digger in the off-season.

John laughed and shook his head. That's bullshit. Who the hell told you that?

I heard it's because of the hole you dig on the mound, Eric said. You know, you always spend like half a hour digging that trench of yours in front of the rubber.

Uh huh, Rick said. It's like a kid at a beach. Sometimes I figure you're getting ready to make a sand castle or something.

Dave laughed, Hey, I think Brainy's on to something.

No, that's not it, either, John said, closing the top of the grill. He returned to the couch and found it occupied with a prone figure. Since he was holding a hamburger in one hand and the tongs in the other, he tried using a foot to shove Eric's legs off his former seat, saying, Hey, where'm I supposed to sit? Move your fat little legs, Eric.

Just when I'm getting comfortable, Eric complained, swinging his legs back in front of him, slouching and folding his hands contently over his stomach. John sat down with a thump and paused to take a big bite of his burger.

Anyways, he said with his mouth half-full, I took some history course when I was a sophomore, or maybe it was fall junior year, I don't remember. Anyway, it was American history or New York State history, I forget which, and I did this paper on the history of the Erie Canal and read in front of the class.

So?

Well, I said that it was called Clinton's Ditch, and that most of the workers who built it were underpaid Irish immigrants. That's who all my ancestors were, all these back hills poor people, all workers with no money. I come from a long line of po' folk, as my father calls them.

So this is where the Ditch came from, huh? Dave leaned forward with a curious expression. So why do you always get pissed off when somebody calls you that?

John took another bite and thought it over. I dunno, he finally said, maybe it's just because...it's just, ah hell, I dunno. It's just, I got a German Jewish last name, and my family's all poor Irish and German and Dutch and English, and every time I visit or hear about all my relatives, it always reminds me that we're all poor, and we're never going to do anything or get anywhere. And every time people call me Ditch, it just reminds me that if I have a family, I'm poor, and if I don't have a family, I don't know who I am.

Remember what you said to Rick about money? Dave asked.

Yeah, I think so. When was that?

You said, That's the dumbest thing I ever heard of.

It's true, you know. I mean, look at you. Look at me. My folks are poor black folks, my father and my grandfather and whoever before him, because before that we don't know who it is. All slaves. And they might as well be slaves now, when you think about it. And you know what?

John lowered the burger to his lap, turned his head questioningly to Dave.

It doesn't matter, Dave said. His eyes were fixed on John's. You know, my people, being black, that's a part of me, that's part of what makes me who I am. But, if I can't get past that, I let the past control my life. You can't live like that, you just can't. You just have to be who you are, who you want to be. That's all. It sounds easy, but it's the hardest thing to do, but once you get there, you have to ask yourself why you thought it was so hard in the first place.

Tell me, o enlightened one...Rick began.

Look, Dave cut in, I'm not saying I'm fine with all this, you know, but it took me a long time to figure out that you can't live in the past. You just can't. You say, Okay, that's what happened, that's why I am who I am right now, but look at all this ahead of me, and what do I want? And then you go get it. If all you do is say, oh, woe is me, then you never do anything but complain about how much life sucks.

You believe in destiny? Eric asked.

What, you mean like our fates have all been chosen and all that?

Yeah, Eric said. Predestination. Nothing we do matters.

No, Dave replied. That's too negative for me, and I don't think it's true anyways. Even if it is true, you can't go around acting like everything you do somebody predicted a billion years ago. You just do what you got to do, with what you got, the best you can. And that's it.

There was a rapping knock on the door. That'll be Mike, John said, getting up. Now, don't everybody freak out here. He's a reporter, but I've known him since high school. He's okay.

We'll behave, dad, Eric said.

John opened the door. Hi, Mike, come on in. We were just discussing free will versus determinism and the existence of God.

Uh huh. How you doing, John? Mike stepped in, dressed down in a short-sleeve button-down shirt with light blue vertical stripes and dark blue jeans. Hey, guys, how's it going.

Hey, the three responded, almost in unison. Mike reached across in front of the TV to shake their hands as John introduced them. This is Eric Holforth, Dave Lawrence, and Rick Reynalds.

Please, be seated, Eric said in a nonchalant snooty voice, turning his head to address John. Jeeves, would you be so kind as to bring in another cold-filtered can for our visitor?

Certainly, sir, John said, bowing slightly at the waist before doing as he was bidden. Would sir like me to kick his ass now or later? and will that be a cold-filtered light or regular piss water?

Make sure to write that down, Dave said to Mike. Make great copy.

Mike laughed. I'm not here to do interviews, just hang out on my lunch break.

You go to work dressed like that? Rick asked.

Hey, I'm a professional. Mike accepted a can and sat on the arm of the couch. What is this we're watching?

The screen showed mustached men in shades and suits running around an apartment complex with rap music in the background. It's nothing, we ain't really watching it, Eric said, grabbing the remote. Lessee if the game's on yet. The screen flipped a few times and landed on a typical camera angle of a pitcher and batter. Behind the home plate area stretched the faded red brick wall of Wrigley Field.

Hey, John, Mike asked, when's the next time you start a home game? Sometime next week?

Hmm, lemme think. I start next Wednesday, and then the Monday after that, so, nope, no starts here next week. Not until whatever date that Monday is. You know, you oughta be asking Dave here when his next start is. He's the guy with the two-point-whatever E.R.A.

Yeah, Dave said. Word.

Mike closed his eyes while counting the days off, then opened them. He said, the 31st, July 31st. Another column the day before that?

Is that a question? John asked.

What do you mean?

Well, we got a deal. A deal's a deal, I'll write one up on time. Don't worry about it.

I know just what you can write about, too, said Rick. You know, I heard...

Eric elbowed him, Not with the press, man. I don't

want him to know about my stash, get it?

Hey, that's pretty funny, guys, Dave said. It's Abbot and Costello come back to life.

The Dynamic Duo, Mike added.

Mork and Mindy, John suggested.

Laverne and Shirley, Mike came back.

Okay, okay, that's where I draw the line, Eric said. I ain't from Milwaukee, and I hate that Twiggy dude.

That gives me an idea, said John. Mike, the *GF News* didn't have like a special pull-out section for Opening Day, did it?

Well, sort of, but I wasn't given enough space to do anything decent. The head honchos told me that what I wanted to do would be in the Wildcats' program anyway.

Then what would you think about interviewing team members, one at a time, and writing up personal backgrounds on them? You know, maybe make up a Player of the Week or something like that.

Hmmm, Mike ruminated. He tipped his can and set it down crushed flat on the floor. You might have something there. Are you volunteering?

Me? John asked. No, I can't do it.

I could pay you for it.

No, no, I can't accept any money. Not during the season. We're not allowed to have another job when we're playing ball. But you should be able to find somebody to do little write-ups once a week, maybe five hundred to a thousand words, you know, get past all the stats and show the fans that there are real people out there on the field.

Yes, Eric put in, dramatically arching a finger at Mike, real people...like you.

He's not real, Rick blurted out. Just look at him! He's an alien!

I like it, said Mike, laughing. I guess I could do it, but I'd rather give it to you. Maybe in the future, huh?

Yeah, John replied, nodding and staring into space for a moment. He swirled the remains of his can and tipped it back.

Right, so, like, I'm first, right? Eric was asking, going into complete camp mode for Mike's benefit. Hi. My name is Eric, and I'm from Memphis, Tennessee. I like biking and video games...

19

It rained all day Monday, July 31st, forcing the cancellation of the Wildcats' night game at home against the Utica Blue Sox. Ditch called his parents from the clubhouse half an hour before the game had been scheduled to start to let them know they shouldn't bother leaving the house. Officially, the umpires had to wait at least half an hour after game time to postpone it, but both teams knew the field conditions would make playing too dangerous. The game was rescheduled for the very next day as part of a twi-night doubleheader starting at 4:30 p.m.

Ditch figured he would miss his turn in the rotation because of the rainout, but Collins told him he'd start the first game of the doubleheader. Some of the players grumbled at the decision to make it two games on the one day; they already were tired out by the hot weather in one game a day, let alone two. Of course, doubleheader games in the minors were only seven innings long, and the rain most likely would lower the temperature some. At least, as the players stripped out of their uniforms in the lockers, soaking wet and dirty even without seeing any play, they all hoped it would be cooler the following day.

The next afternoon turned out to be even more humid than the previous, however, with the temperature expected to hit 94 degrees by 2 or 3 o'clock. Ditch threw about twenty pitches an hour before game time and rested in the dugout, talking with Holforth about the opposing team's batters. He tried not to think about his parents, who undoubtedly would come to the game. His father had no qualms about leaving early from work, but he wasn't so sure it was a good idea for his mother to bring his sister Jennifer to the ballpark on such a hot day. And his mother would *have* to bring Jennifer if she came to the game; she was so desperately protective of the five-year-old that she refused to trust any babysitter. Ditch hoped there wouldn't be trouble at the front gate like last time. His mother had tried to bring in a small cooler and a container of iced tea, and it was only the divine intervention of one of the team coaches that prevented the confiscation of the offending items.

The sun was still high overhead when Ditch ascended the mound to start the top of the first. A slightly larger than normal crowd of almost three thousand had come to the park, encouraged by Mike Grant's preview of the appearance of the local "star" and the prospect of seeing two games for the price of one. The increased volume of crowd noise initially startled Ditch, but as he settled into a fast pitching groove, the noise of vendors calling out their wares and small children shrieking and Little Leaguers charging in wolf packs after foul balls all seemed to blend into a low distant rumbling murmur at the back of his head. The sun beat down on his sun-screen protected neck and he pitched through the first three innings with no trouble at all, facing the minimum of nine batters.

The game was moving past him quickly that late afternoon. The sun began to dip towards the horizon, casting shadows of the vacant outfield bleachers across the still damp grass. It would take a while for the shadows to reach the lip of the infield dirt, but to Ditch the shadows seemed to lengthen visibly feet at a time. Time passed quickly, much too quickly, as he worked his way through the fourth, walking and stranding one batter. He had three strikeouts already, which he thought was a record for him in one game this season. The sun seemed to beat down even harder with each passing inning, though he knew it was slowly setting. The humidity slowly increased, he had sweated clean through his uniform shirt and his blue belt had turned a blackish-purple. The fan set up to blow air along the floor of the dugout might as well not have even been there, for all the good it did. But Ditch didn't mind the heat. He felt stronger, and knew his sinker would continue dropping with each visit to the mound. The crowd was humming to him.

After the fifth inning, the Wildcats had the lead two to nothing. Ditch allowed an infield error and another walk in the top of the inning, but a groundball and a pop out erased the scoring threat. He returned to the dugout, and when he sat, the other players avoided him. Burying his face in a wet towel, Ditch dragged it over his head and let it rest around the base of his neck and across his shoulders. No one would talk to him. Holforth chose a seat near Collins, at the habitual roost at the bat rack. Ditch felt inclined to glance at the scoreboard, but successfully resisted the temptation. *No*, he thought, *think about something else. It's a Zen thing. Focus on not focusing.*

After five innings, he had a no-hitter. And he knew that everyone in the park knew it. He forced himself to concentrate on the next three batters. So far through five he'd faced a total of eighteen batters, everyone in the order twice apiece. He'd gotten the first batter due up in the sixth on slow curveballs outside; the second one popped up and grounded out on the sinker; and the third grounded out twice, once to third on a change and once to second on a fastball inside. Ditch was confident he could repeat the pitches if need be, depending upon the ball count. His fastball wasn't as fast as he wanted it to be, but even at only 80 miles an hour or so, the movement he was getting made it appear much faster, especially after a curve or change.

It continued to work in the sixth, as he set them down one-two-three, all on ground outs. Holforth hadn't come out to the mound to talk since the fourth, which had been an extremely brief trip anyway, but his pitch-calling had been nearly flawless. Ditch was pitching easily and quickly, his fastball had zip and pop on it, and the sinker combined with well-placed changeups were completely fooling the batters. The location of the sun in the sky told him it couldn't possibly be earlier than six or seven o'clock, but he felt as if it were still the beginning of the afternoon. The flags on the foul poles were still, but the stands behind home plate were not. A steady cadence of rhythmic stamping started during the Wildcats' half of the sixth inning, the increasing volume of activity shaking the dugout. The crowd knew the minor league rules: each game of the doubleheader would last only seven innings. Three outs to go.

Ditch could feel the pulse of the crowd through the concrete floor, up through his cleated feet and the polyester of his pants. His eyes darted across the field, examining every aspect of the field itself, seeking out the creeping shadows spreading the wavering outline of the stands and light towers across the infield. Soon it would touch the mound, and the lights which had already been turned on would begin to affect the fielders. He hoped the effect of the ball coming out of the shadows towards home plate would appear to make his pitches jump out at the batter from nowhere. *Only one more inning*, he thought. *One more.*

In contrast to the tumult of the crowd, the Wildcats' dugout in the sixth inning was silent as stone. Letting his jacket lay neglected on the bench, Ditch closed his eyes and prayed for a rally, prayed for an extension of time resting on the bench. *Please, please*, he prayed to his teammates preparing in the on deck circle, *load the bases, get extra-base hits, start a fight. Anything.*

Three up and down. The Blue Sox had changed pitchers, and the new reliever was effective. The score remained two-nothing. The shaking stands roared as the Wildcats took the field for the top of the seventh. Still sitting on the bench, Ditch watched the glove slip onto his hand, rubbed his fingertips against the raised laces along the outside thumb, where the faded black magic marker spelled out his name in two inch-high letters. He pulled his cap back on and slowly headed for the mound. After taking ten pitches, Ditch walked around the mound, squeezing life into the ball with both hands. Sweat was trickling down his cheeks from his temples, and he let it run as he faced the plate and saw a multi-colored sea rise to greet him. The sun stopped its pounding at his back and seemed to envelop him instead, a warm tingling sensation crawling rapidly up his pitching arm from fingers on the seams to elbow to shoulder. The first batter stepped in.

Number 8, the cleanup batter, had flied out to left in the first and popped out to short to end the fourth. He was a big guy, maybe six-three or six-four, looked about 220 pounds, maybe more. But Ditch knew the Sox had been told to take pitches, because they needed runners. Holforth signaled for a fastball down the middle, inside. Ditch obliged, and as it headed towards the batter's midriff and cut back across the inside corner, the umpire threw his hand up for a strike call. The crowd roared its approval. Holforth immediately signaled for a sinker low and inside, and the batter fouled it into the Wildcats' bullpen, sending metal chairs scattering across the grass. The next pitch was a slow change outside, but the batter wouldn't bite, checking his swing as it fell well outside the strike zone. Ditch got the ball back and let his arms fall limp at his sides as he stared in from the shadows.

The catcher signed for another change, outside. He apparently had decided that the batter would eventually go for it. Ditch shook his head, and then nodded, without Holforth having changed the call. With any luck, the batter might second-guess himself. The pitch traveled the same path as the previous one, with the same result. With the count 2 and 2, Ditch knew the next pitch was crucial. A full count coming from an oh-2 count was a big psychological advantage for the batter. This time the curve was called for, back across the inside corner, waist high. The pitch sailed on him, and the batter raised his hands up and watched the ball stay waist-high inside. The full count had come unwanted, and now the batter had the advantage. The crowd noise rose to a near-fever pitch as Ditch received the signs. Holforth wanted the curve again, same spot, a bit lower. Ditch hesitated, thinking about shaking it off, then changed his mind and nodded. The pitch curved around towards the outstretched glove, but the batter fouled it away just in time, bouncing it straight down and back, catching a piece of the umpire's left foot and skidding towards the home on deck circle. Time was called as the umpire walked around for a moment, testing his foot.

The sun no longer rested on Ditch's neck, having half-disappeared behind the right field bleachers. He stayed on the mound, brushing away dirt from the rubber with his foot, holding the ball in his glove and rotating the seams for a fastball grip. Number 8's bat had been slowed down by now, so the time was appropriate for a little zinger.

When the umpire settled himself behind the catcher

again, Holforth had evidently read his pitcher's mind, calling for a fastball low and outside. If the batter hit it, unless he had incredible opposite-field strength, it would either be a ground out to the right side of the infield, or he would try to pull it and wind up popping out to the left side. Ditch unwound and zipped it across the plate, too low. The batter dropped his bat on the plate and bounded to first with a walk, Ditch's third of the game. The crowd hushed momentarily, but gathered strength again as the second batter of the inning stepped in.

Number 23 had grounded out once and struck out once, on a sinker in the dirt. The righty seemed to like the ball low, which went against the grain a bit, but since he had gone after pitches in the dirt, Holforth seemed to think he would do so again. The first pitch, a sinker, came in low and inside, but the batter didn't swing. Ball one. Ditch glanced over his left shoulder. Reynalds was holding the runner on at first, but the big man didn't seem much of a running threat. He barely had an arm's length lead at first and rested his hands on his knees, staring at the pitcher.

Holforth called for another sinker, almost the same location but a bit more over the plate. Ditch checked the runner at first and threw.

The crack of the bat resounded throughout the park. Ditch turned around and stood motionless as the ball landed between the left and center fielders and slid into and off of the base of the wall. The runner hustled as fast as he could around second, but the center fielder's throw came in quickly enough to keep him from scoring. The batter pulled up at second with a stand-up double.

A hush settled over Ditch's senses, and he heard the words in his head before speaking them out loud. "I've failed," he said.

He leaned forward, bent at the waist, resting his hands on his knees and repeated the words. "I've failed." He looked up to the scoreboard and saw a series of bright lights form the number one under the visitor's hit column. He felt an arm around his shoulders, Holforth's, but he stood there, staring at the scoreboard, oblivious. "I've failed," he said again, not able to get the words out of his mind.

"What are you talking about, Ditch?" he heard Holforth shout. The catcher turned him around to face the crowd. He looked up at Holforth's dirt-streaked face, catcher's mask drawn back over his hard hat.

"Look at them," the catcher said. "Listen to them. Do you think they care?"

Ditch looked up to the stands. The crowd was on their collective feet, and it slowly dawned on him that they were giving him a standing ovation. Sound returned to his ears, and it was the sound of clapping thunder.

"Ditch," he heard from his right. His manager approached, hands in his pants pockets, somehow appearing freshly pressed after an afternoon in the sun and humid air. "Are you all right?" Collins asked.

Ditch nodded. He felt the ball in his glove and kicked at the mound, trying to shake himself awake. "Do you want to stay in?" Collins asked him. At Ditch's slow nod, he patted the pitcher on the shoulder and said, "Finish it," before returning to the dugout and making a call to get bullpen activity.

The crowd slowly sat down and quieted a bit as the next batter stepped to the plate. Ditch removed his cap and wiped his forehead with a sleeve. The batter lined the first pitch straight up the middle, scoring both runners. Ditch found himself on one knee behind the mound, resting his forehead on his forearm, listening to nothing. He heard nothing at all until Kriek arrived to stall for time. After a few more minutes, Collins came out and asked for the ball as a reliever came in. Ditch quietly trudged towards the dugout, and was awakened by a tap to the shoulder; it was White, returning as his reliever, telling him not to worry, that everything was under control. Ditch slowed and tried to smile. White opened his mouth to shout something at him. Ditch didn't know why he was shouting. The word "cap" appeared in front of him for some reason. He felt White move away, towards the mound, and he slowly removed his sweat-soaked cap and raised it to the sky.

In the bottom of the eighth, Reynald's bloop single over the second baseman's head into short right field plated the winning run as the reddening clouds spread across the lower foothills of the Adirondacks to the western skyline. Ditch received a no-decision, and White got the win, his fourth of the season, his first in relief. There was an hour break to turn the lights all the way on and rest the teams a bit, and the second game started.

20

The sun was still high in the sky, partially hiding behind a late afternoon cumulus coverage, casting moving shadows over the empty ballpark. John and his father entered from an old chain link gate to the left of the home dugout and wandered around the field slowly, walking across the third base coach's box to the pitcher's mound. The stands were filled with bits of paper, remains of cardboard beer cup holders and red striped popcorn boxes, straw wrappings and an occasional baseball cap or T-shirt accidentally left behind by the fans on Fan Appreciation Day, the first Friday of September, the last game of the Class A season in Gladden Fords.

John's mother stood on the other side of the fence, behind the refastened gate, holding Jennifer on her hip and looking out at father and son. John had asked if she wanted to join them, but she had decided to remain in the stands, an observer, his final fan.

The two stood behind the mound, John in shorts and tank top, his father still sporting good pants and shirt and tie from the office. They stood there quietly for a moment or two, watching the grounds crew of one take one last mowing ride through the outfield. When he was done, he would escort them off the field, exit the ballpark, and lock the doors behind him, until the next spring came around.

John's father asked him whether he would be pitching again. John said he didn't know. He was tempted to stand on the mound again, to toe the rubber and pretend his catcher still squatted behind the plate.

I'm sorry, Dad, he said to the wind. I wanted to make you proud, and I just screwed up again. I'm sorry.

You always make me proud, his father replied, not a trace of condescension or patronizing tone in his voice. You make me proud because you're my oldest son.

John turned and looked at his father, for a moment, trying to see past the deepening ridges above his eyebrows and the thinning whiteness of his beard and mustache, through the dull gray of his sun-sensitive glasses, for the truth in the statement. All he saw was his father. Dad, I...

He paused and looked back to the stands, still resisting the desire to climb the mound a last time, melodramatically. You know, I look at the box score the next day, after I pitch, all it tells me is the statistics. I don't see any thought in there, or any sweat, or any frustration. All I see are numbers. Is that what it all boils down to?

He looked back to his father. Is there anything more? If I write something, will anyone understand?

You were there, his father said. I was there, your mother and sister were there. All those people were there, the whole season. We know what happened, and nothing else matters. What do you think's more important, what's on paper, he asked, tapping his temple, or what's in here?

John lowered his head. Yeah, I suppose so, he said. He shook his head, trying to remember. I just wish it had lasted longer, he said. I wish I could go back and do it again, and savor just that one moment.

John's father smiled. You can, he said. You always can.

The two stood there a moment longer. John could see the riding mower closing its loops as it scraped the infield dirt, shooting up small clouds of dust in its wake. He glanced up at the figure standing over the right field wall; the rough rider didn't sag in his saddle, but he rattled with the wind, the metallic surface at last failing to disguise the flawed structure beneath. A proud visage, and suddenly John was reminded of his grandfather, dark-furrowed forehead, hunched over a breakfast of a bowl of hot milk covering a brick of shredded wheat. Defiance, of a different sort, and yet the same as it had ever been. He tore his glance away and sent his gaze circling the field and stands before dropping to his feet. John looked up. We better get going, he said to his father, who nodded. I hear Craig and Lisa are in town for Labor Day weekend.

That's right, his father replied, as they began the slow walk back to the gate.

What about the others? John asked.

Well, his father said, Luke's just starting his MBA program at Albany, Brian and Ben drove up there to Plattsburgh last Monday when you were out in Jamestown. I wish Brian had gone to Oneonta like I told him, because I think Ben's a bad influence on him, but Ben's showing more maturity lately, so maybe things'll work out.

Yeah.

It's because of you, you know, his father said. You were the trailblazer for the rest of your siblings.

C'mon, Dad, John said, that's not true. Whatever they all did, they did on their own. I didn't help them, they did it themselves. With some help from you and Mom, of course, even if they don't say so.

Even if they don't say so, his father agreed. Whatever the case, you were the first. You always will be.

I know, John said, sighing. I know.

They reached the gate, and John's mother immediately handed Jennifer to her husband, saying, I'm tired from holding her, you take her.

Is that all I'm good for? John's father asked.

Yep, John's mother replied. She'll be too big to hold in a little while.

In a little while, huh, John's father said. They walked up the concrete steps between rows of blue plastic seats on the left side and wooden bleachers on the right. Their steps quietly slapped against the concrete surface and echoed slightly once inside the roofed pavilion area, heading out towards the gravel parking lot.

So, what are you going to do now, John? his mother asked him.

Well, I thought I'd go out to dinner with you all and then head on over to the Holiday Inn for our team party. They're all taking off tomorrow.

I mean for a living, John. What are you going to do? Are you going to work for your father?

Um, I don't know, John answered neutrally. I might have his job after a while, so I'd rather, you know, take it easy on him. His father chuckled.

I don't know, John continued, in a bit more serious tone. Mike's been offering me a job at the newspaper, I may take him up on it. I don't know too much about anything but baseball, but I guess I could learn.

Whatever you do, I'm sure you'll do it well, his father said, stopping to lower Jennifer to the ground. She stomped her feet as if revving up her engines and took off for the turnstiles. She chose one to the left of the line of six, and it refused to turn at her energetic pushes. Jennifer, honey, John's mother called, they don't go that way. The three caught up with her quickly. John's mother redirected his little sister over to the right, and happily Jennifer pushed her way through to the other side, almost hitting herself in the back of the head with the turnstile's metal bars.

You know, John said as they walked towards the lone car in the parking lot, his mother's old tan Caprice Classic. I've been thinking about writing. I've had this idea for a story in the back of my mind.

What kind of story? his father asked, buckling Jennifer into a seat in the back. Here, you can get in the front, John. Your legs are longer than mine.

Okay. Well, I'm not really sure what kind of story it would be. I've just been thinking. It's kinda hokey, but I could write this baseball story, about a writer who always wanted to play baseball.

Hmmm, well, his father said, you never know, it could work. I say go for it. What have you got to lose?

Yeah, John said. His mother clambered into the front seat and flipped her hair behind her as she gunned the engine. Where are we going, straight home? John asked.

Well, his father started.

We'll meet Lisa and her husband and Craig at home, his mother interrupted, and then we can go out to a Denny's or a Friendly's. If your father has the money.

If I have the money, John's father said. In that case, Friendly's, here we come.

John's mother angled the car to the left, towards the parking lot exit. John rolled his window all the way and stuck his right elbow out it, looking back at the receding ballpark. The sun remained hidden behind the clouds, and as they drove away, there were no shadows to stretch out behind them.

About the Author

Originally from Troy, New York, M. Thomas Apple spent part of his childhood in the tiny hamlet of Berne in the Helderbergs of Albany Country and his teenage years in the slightly larger village of Warrensburg in the Adirondacks. He played high school baseball for four years and was a decent base-stealer, adequate outfielder, and terrible batter. Occasionally he dreams about the sole (running) homerun he hit on a 3-0 count, and the subsequent beaning that followed during the next at-bat.

He studied languages and literature as an undergraduate student at Bard College and later creative writing at the University of Notre Dame. After further studies at Temple University, he now teaches global issues and English as a second language at Ritsumeikan University in Kyoto, Japan. He lives in a house co-designed with his wife and partially decorated by his two daughters, nestled in the foothills of the mountains and surrounded by lots and lots of Japanese cedar and cicada.

Approaching Twi-Night is his first novel. A book of his non-fiction essays (*Taking Leave: An American on Paternity Leave in Japan*, Perceptia Press) is scheduled for publication in late 2015, followed by collection of short fiction and poetry (*Notes from the Nineties*) in early 2016.